DEATH IN WILLOW PATTERN

DEATH IN WILLOW PATTERN

by

W. J. BURLEY

Walker and Company • New York

First published in the United States of America in 1970
by the Walker Publishing Company, Inc.

Library of Congress Catalog Card Number: 73-98011

Printed in the United States of America from type set in
Great Britain.

Know ye the willow-tree
   Whose grey leaves quiver,
Whispering gloomily
   To yon pale river?
Lady, at eventide
   Wander not near it:
They say its branches hide
   A sad lost spirit!

W. M. Thackeray: *The Willow Tree*

My thanks are due to Dr. F. A. Turk for indispensable help with the sections which concern Chinese art.

CHAPTER ONE

A MELANCHOLY NOVEMBER day, rain drizzling out
of a leaden sky, the harbour and the village beyond a study
in greys. Fog in the Channel; a muffled blast on the signal
at Chapel Point every thirty seconds. The surface of the
harbour gleaming dully like a mirror faintly misted, the
boats still, and ghostly as their reflections. The few remaining
Gurnick fishermen gathered sociably in their loft, mending
gear and gossiping, the quayside loafers huddled in a shelter.
November the twenty-fifth.

Dr. Henry Pym stood at his window staring out over the
harbour while he dictated to his secretary.

'With regard to the elaborate sculpturing of the prothoracic
tergum, no doubt ingenious and ingenuous attempts will
be made to assign to it some adaptive significance. In the
opinion of the present writer, such effort might, with equal
justification and profit, be devoted to the liberal embellish-
ments on the Albert Memorial . . .'

'You can't say that, Henry!'

'Why not? It's perfectly true.'

Susan, his secretary, swept blonde hair back from her forehead in a gesture of impatience. 'They wouldn't print it—it's
journalese and cheap at that.'

'I think it's rather good—leave it in.'

Susan might have carried the argument further but she was
interrupted by a bell ringing in some distant part of the house.
'The front door bell, I'd better answer it, there's nobody else
in.'

She went and Pym continued to stand by the window. The
huge single sheet of glass gave him a panoramic view of the
village and harbour. He could see dimly through the mist

the water-front, the quay, the fish cellars converted into shops and the pyramid of little houses rising up the hill behind. His own house, built into the side of a low promontory, rose sheer out of the water so that the harbour traffic passed right under his windows. In the season he was one of the sights to be pointed out to trippers along with the seals on White Island, the wreck of *M.V. Gladiator* and a distant prospect of six church steeples on a clear day. The lucky ones saw a tall, lean, slightly stooping figure and they might even notice the extreme pallor of his features.

'Dr. Henry Pym, writer and criminologist, working in his study. His house, *The Labyrinth*, so called after the palace of King Minos of Crete, was built by Dr. Pym on the site of an ancient chapel believed to mark the spot where St. Petroc landed after a miraculous crossing from Ireland on a granite quern.'

Then the boat's engines which had been throttled back would be accelerated. 'Now we are passing through the harbour heads for the open sea. On the port side . . .'

Pym secretly enjoyed it as he enjoyed any publicity which did not interfere too much with his convenience. He would even stand in the window when the boats were due though he professed to be irritated. 'We shall have to move, Susan,' he would say. 'I came here for peace and quiet and I find myself like a goldfish in a bowl. I am not only on show, I am positively *exhibited*.'

Susan came back. 'The post—two recorded deliveries among the rest.'

Pym took the envelopes, perched on the edge of his desk to slit them open. He glanced through the contents before putting them on one side; one letter he read through and remarked without obvious relevance, 'A month to Christmas, Susan.'

'So I believe.'

'How would you like to spend it with the landed gentry?'

'Is somebody offering?'

He passed the letter over. 'Sir Francis Leigh of *Peel Place*.'

A letter written in the gentleman's own spidery hand on thick embossed paper:

8

'My Dear Dr. Pym,

I am presuming on a brief acquaintance (the occasion of which has probably passed from your memory) to beg a favour. It is that you will advise me in the disposal of certain books and manuscripts in my library which I believe to be of scientific as well as of antiquarian value and interest. My ancestor, Joseph Leigh, who succeeded to *Peel* in 1766 at the age of seventeen, became an enthusiastic amateur naturalist and in the course of his long life he built up a collection of works on various aspects of natural philosophy and exchanged letters with many like-minded persons both in this country and abroad. His son, Roger and his grandsons, Edward and John, inherited his interests and enthusiasms so that the material to which I refer was accumulated over three generations.

Let me say at once that my interest in its disposal is not a pecuniary one. If any of the books or manuscripts are of importance, I shall be glad to present them to any institution of your choosing.

I realize, of course, that if you humour me you will be undertaking a troublesome and time-consuming task but my very temerity may help to assure you that I am not without hope that your labours will prove rewarding. If you decide to give me the benefit of your advice, I leave the time to you. I will merely say, that Christmas is a month away and it may be that you would care to spend it with us.

In the hope that we are about to improve our acquaintance, I remain,

Sincerely yours,
Francis Leigh.'

Pym watched her read. 'Tempting, isn't it? Think! His collection must cover the century from 1770 to 1870—the golden age of the amateur. If his ancestors really knew their stuff it could be important.'
'You want to go?'
'If I don't, he'll get some dealer with an axe to grind.'

9

'At Christmas?'

'It seems as good a time as any other. Will you come?'

Susan laughed. 'I only work here! But I've no objection to a little mingling with the gentry if the food is good and the beds are comfortable.'

So the arrangements were made; they were committed.

As Christmas drew nearer, so Henry regarded the prospect of their visit with increasing distaste, but this was usual; he would enter cheerfully into social engagements then rail against fate as the time of fulfilment approached. But on the twenty-third of December, another still, wet, foggy day, they set out for *Peel Place*, an estate on the outskirts of the county town. The car behaved badly, failing to develop full power and breasting every rise with what seemed to be an incredulous sigh of relief. Henry, who never drove himself, and denied all knowledge of mechanical things, sat beside Susan bemoaning the unreliability of motor vehicles and foretelling a five mile walk to the nearest garage. Susan, rapidly losing patience, pointed out that the car had never given a moment's trouble in three years and added, 'But if you feel like that about it, I suggest you trade it in for a horse.'

Peel Place was on the other side of the town and Susan had to coax the temperamental car through streets almost choked with Christmas shoppers and their parked cars. At every halt the engine died and following cars hooted their impatience. There seemed to be more than the usual quota of policemen about but they, fortunately, were superior to traffic problems. A steep hill out of town made them hold their breaths, a level stretch for a mile, and they were there; at least, they were at the gates. Impressive gates with massive stone gateposts each surmounted by the weathered figure of a standing bear, carved in stone.

'The Vane bears,' Henry said. He could be relied upon to do his homework. 'Nothing to do with the Leighs. The Vanes were the original owners and the Leighs bought them out in 1730. Upstarts.' A Lilliputian lodge and a drive which followed a sinuous course between screens of rhododendron then opened into a large area of parkland with the house on rising

10

ground against a background of elms. A modest house, to the Queen Anne recipe, hipped roof, corniced eaves, dormer windows; charming. An anticlimax after the entrance and the long drive.

'Built as a dower house,' Henry informed her. 'The Tudor mansion was largely destroyed by fire in the eighteen forties. Edward Leigh moved in here and had the ruin demolished.'

Broad steps, gleaming in the rain, between sweeping balustrades, led up to a double front door with a shell canopy. Unfamiliar ground to Susan, bred in a London suburb. Was that why she felt uneasy? Late afternoon and the dusk beginning to steal away the doleful grey light of the day; the rain falling in a fine mist without a breath of wind; and silence. Henry pulled at the heavy brass lever of the door bell and waited. Footsteps on stone flags, the sound of a latch being lifted and the door opened. Sir Francis himself.

A short rotund figure of almost Pickwickian proportions; dark but greying hair fringing a broad shining patch of baldness. His brown eyes mild, wondering, looked out through old-fashioned spectacles with thin gold rims and quite circular lenses. His chubby features readily creased into smiles and he laughed often. Susan, who expected a lean thin-lipped aristocrat, thought that this little roly-poly man would have looked more at home behind a grocery counter, but his manner was engaging and before long she was telling him of their troubles with the car. He listened attentively.

'I expect it's choked jets. I don't know what they are but that is what I was told when I had similar trouble. Fortunately it appears to be a relatively inexpensive malady. If you leave the key I will ask Harold to get it attended to.'

He introduced them to his married daughter, Lucy North. Jet black straight hair in a business-like bob; a well-worn woollen jumper suit and sensible shoes. She couldn't be more than thirty but her dumpy little figure and her matronly air made her seem older. Her eyes fascinated Susan; they seemed to be immobile, conveying an impression of serenity or of detachment, perhaps of indifference.

'My wife died when Lucy was born and she keeps house.

Her husband Gerald is a local solicitor, a fact which I find extremely useful.'

Lucy showed them to their rooms, in the front of the house. No Queen Anne plumbing, a modern bathroom opening off each bedroom; central heating. Lucy stayed while Susan unpacked, it was embarrassing to be watched by those calm inscrutable eyes.

'You must make yourself at home; we don't stand on ceremony.'

'Thanks, I will.'

Silence that lengthened.

'It will be nice having you here, we see very little company.'

Susan tried to think of something to say but failed.

'I hope you stay a long time.' The words came in a little rush as though from a child who has plucked up courage.

Susan smiled as sweetly as she knew how and said, 'How kind you are!' And meant it. She felt sorry for this dowdy little woman who seemed so anxious for companionship. Then she happened to glance out of the window and saw someone examining their car. It was getting dark but the light was enough for her to make out a seemingly giant figure in overalls, a figure almost as broad as it was long. 'Who's that?'

Lucy looked and laughed. 'It's only Johnny—Johnny Vane. He's found your car, it doesn't take him long to spot a stranger.' She sat on the bed, glad to have found a subject of conversation. 'Johnny's father is the agent for the estate, they live in one of the houses; charming people. But poor Johnny is a deaf mute, almost unteachable but quite harmless—lovable really. Only two things interest him, birds and motor cars . . .'

'How sad!'

'Yes, I suppose it is. It's certainly sad for his father, but Johnny seems happy enough.' She paused so that Susan, in the act of hanging a dress in the wardrobe, turned to look at her and met once again her disturbing, persistent gaze. 'Sometimes I think Johnny is not so badly off, I mean, a great deal passes over his head and nobody expects anything of him.'

12

'Vane—isn't that the name of the original owners of the estate? Are they the same family or is it a coincidence?'

A moment of hesitation. 'Oh, they are the same family, but it's also something of a coincidence that they should be here. Some years ago when father advertised for an agent, Harold applied and got the job. His people were farmers in quite a big way and Harold was brought up to farming but he quarrelled with his father and cleared off to Malaya—rubber planting or something; then when the trouble started there he more or less had to come home. Like a good many other returning empire builders, he found himself out of a job.'

A slightly scornful note but whether it was personal to Harold Vane or an attitude to short-term emigrants, Susan was uncertain. She was beginning to wonder whether she would have to bath and dress under her supervision when Lucy stood up. 'I must leave you to change. I'm afraid you'll find me an incurable gossip but it's so nice to have someone to talk to.'

At the door she paused, 'Your Doctor Pym—isn't he a criminologist?'

'I suppose you could call him that. He is primarily a zoologist but he has written several books and articles on the psychology of crime.'

Lucy nodded. 'I thought so.' Like so many other people who talk a great deal when they feel like it, she was able to break off a conversation with disconcerting abruptness. She went out, closing the door behind her.

Susan bathed and put on a simple short-sleeved Tricel dress which she hoped would be acceptable evening wear in the Leigh household, then she went downstairs.

Henry and Francis Leigh were in the drawing-room with a third man whom Susan had not yet met. Lucy's husband, Gerald North, the solicitor. He was much more the lean thin-lipped aristocrat of Susan's imagining, his movements were restrained and his manner reserved and he was at least ten years older than Lucy.

As Susan could have guessed, Henry was doing most of the talking and he allowed himself to be interrupted only while

13

Sir Francis introduced her to his son-in-law and provided her with sherry.

'I expect Lucy has told you that we have a meal at seven-thirty which we call supper.'

Henry sat, elegantly relaxed in a winged-back chair, apparently studying the refracted light from the chandelier through the facets of his sherry glass. Susan recognized what the zoologist calls cryptic behaviour—fitting into the surroundings—stick insects (*Phasmidae*) and certain moths, for example the Chinese Character Moth (*Cilix*), do it extremely well and so did Henry. Her only concern was the risk that he might parody the part but then she remembered that this particular *milieu* must be nearer to his natural habitat than most.

'If human societies are to survive, the conflict between social needs and individual aspirations must be resolved. It is of no help to pretend that there is no such conflict, it is, in my opinion the central problem of politics. On the one hand there are the advocates of extreme *laissez-faire*, those who hold to the Benthamite dictum that the most useful function of government is to be quiet. On the other hand there are the Marxists who believe that the individual must subserve the state in every aspect of his being. In practice, most political organizations, whatever they profess, gravitate to a position somewhere between the two.'

Henry paused to sip his sherry and to allow his point to be taken, but Sir Francis interrupted. 'You are certainly right about political parties. I am an incorrigible individualist and that is an extremely unfashionable thing to be when even our so-called right wing Tories are no more than pink liberals!'

Susan was surprised to see the chubby features flush and the brown eyes sparkle.

Obviously a warm topic. 'But surely, Dr. Pym, as a biologist, you must recognize that the natural state of society is one of unfettered competition. I understand that Darwin formulated his evolutionary theory on the basis of what he observed to take place in nature—a struggle for existence resulting in

14

the survival of the fittest. That is Nature's way and it will have to be ours, whatever the political theorists have to say about it.'

Susan knew that this little speech had accurately plumbed Sir Francis's intellectual depth to Henry's satisfaction. His manner became even more that of a tolerant tutor addressing a dull-witted undergraduate. 'Nature, I am afraid, is like holy writ, Sir Francis, capable of witnessing to almost any proposition. But it would be a mistake to seek her support for a society based on individualism. The most complex animal societies, those of insects, are conformist to a degree which makes the most rigid Marxist society imaginable seem irresponsibly permissive.'

Gerald North had not spoken hitherto, now he set his sherry glass down on the tray, patted his lips with a spotlessly white handkerchief and addressed himself to Henry. 'Are you saying that the lesson to be learned from nature is a Marxist one?'

Henry uncrossed his long legs and shifted a little uncomfortably in his chair. 'That is a very difficult question. In biological terms the test of success is survival and in the long view that must also be the test of our success.' Henry hesitated, an unusual phenomenon. 'I think I must answer your question in this way: the more complex our society becomes, the greater the need for individual restraint, either voluntary or imposed. This is saying nothing very profound, it simply means that a complicated mechanism is more easily upset than a simple one.'

'So that if we are to increase the measure of individual freedom our society must be simplified—is that it?'

Henry shook his head. 'Not entirely, for complexity in social organization seems to be a function of size. There are too many of us—far too many.' He smiled, struck by a whimsical notion. 'Perhaps freedom is a limited commodity after all, the further it has to go, the thinner it must be spread. Come to think of it, that is not such an absurd idea, it may well be justifiable on mathematical grounds.'

Gerald North placed the tips of his long white fingers together and studied them. 'So that Huxley's *Brave New World* and Orwell's *1984* are not to be taken as threats or as warnings but rather as descriptive of an inevitable stage in our social evolution?'

Henry was unaccustomed to having his conversational ventures pinned out and labelled but he conceded the point. 'Allowing for dramatic licence, I think that is probably true.'

Sir Francis sat on the very edge of his chair, his hands clasped about his knees, looking like a plump benevolent gnome. He laughed. 'You scientists are all the same. You see clearly the inevitable consequences of folly but you are unwilling to do anything about it. You speak of the menace of overpopulation, a situation which is a consequence of gratuitous interference with natural checks and balances, with the mechanism of the struggle for existence. Yet in every cultural backwater of the world your science is still striving to preserve and lengthen life without regard for its merit; you are deliberately frustrating the process of natural selection and the price will be paid one day.'

Henry was looking at Sir Francis with renewed interest. 'Then what do you suggest? Are you proposing a deliberate curtailment of humanitarian effort in underdeveloped countries?'

'Humanitarian! That is the magic word, the blanket which covers every piece of quixotic sentimentality from ideas on racial equality to the abolition of capital punishment. The point is that in the not very distant future we have to face, in fact we have to secure, a drastic reduction in world population. Is this to be indiscriminate or is it to be a culling out of those who have demonstrated their inaptitude for survival by their failure to secure a place in the main stream of human progress?'

Not such a benevolent gnome. But did he really believe in this vicious nonsense? Susan was incredulous though each time he had spoken she had seen his genial features harden, his cheeks flush. Heinrich Himmler had a reputation as an amiable husband and an affectionate father.

'Make no mistake, Dr. Pym, the law of the jungle is still the ethic of survival. *Die Natur hat jederzeit Recht.*'

16

Lucy North had come in in time to hear her father's last remark. Susan saw mingled anxiety and tenderness in the look which she gave him and saw too his quick reassuring smile.

'When father starts quoting Goethe it usually means that he is well and truly astride his hobby horse. Fortunately he doesn't mean the half of it but perhaps it's as well that supper is ready.' She turned again to her father, 'Harold is here and I've persuaded him to stay for supper. He's ringing up Helen.'

'Harold Vane,' Sir Francis explained, 'is agent for the estate—and a lot of other things. I don't know what we would do without him.'

It was a very ordinary meal; plain food, well enough cooked and served. They were waited upon by a white-faced middle-aged spinsterish woman whom they called Flossie and who seemed to be almost one of the family.

Harold Vane was the outdoor type; tweeds and a checked shirt with a bright red tie. He was stocky with broad open features, his skin with a smooth brown patina, his hair bleached almost white. Susan liked him on sight.

'I took the liberty of running your car into Marsden's where we have all our estate work done. It seems to me the timing is all adrift and they have a pretty good electrician there.'

'That was extremely good of you . . .'

'Not at all, I had to go in to pick up one of our Land Rovers. But it's Christmas Eve tomorrow and what you don't get done then may have to wait some time. We can collect it tomorrow afternoon sometime.'

They ate in silence for a while. Sir Francis sat at the head of the table wielding his knife and fork with gusto and smiling at anyone who caught his eye. Gerald North was not served with the same food as the others, he had tomato juice instead of soup, steamed fish instead of the meat course and while the others drank claret he had only water. He sat, bolt upright, his eyes scarcely ever lifting from his food and he ate with quick precise movements which seemed to enhance rather than destroy the illusion of immobility. He had not spoken since the brief exchange with Henry in the drawing-room.

'Gerald nurses an ulcer; they have been boon companions for years.'

North made not the slightest acknowledgment of this dubious pleasantry and the others felt uncomfortable. Harold Vane helped himself to more claret. 'Our poison-pen friend has been at it again, then.'

Lucy's knife and fork clattered on to her plate. 'Oh, no!'

A prolonged silence while Harold looked round the table realizing that he had dropped a large-sized brick. 'I thought it was agreed that we should ask Dr. Pym's advice.'

Gerald cleared his mouth, patted his lips with a napkin and spoke chidingly, 'That is so, Harold, but since Dr. Pym arrived only a few hours ago, a suitable opportunity has not yet arisen.'

Harold flushed. 'I'm sorry.'

Sir Francis turned to Henry, 'We owe you our apologies. Since your visit was arranged we, that is to say Harold, Gerald and I, have received poison-pen letters and we had agreed to ask your advice as to what action, if any, we should take.'

Susan was aware of a marked coolness in Henry's reply. 'I imagine that Mr. North's professional advice would be of far more value.'

North laughed, a dry cackling sound. '"Physician, heal thyself!"—good advice but extremely difficult to follow. One's own problems are always special cases.'

'I should really be most grateful for your opinion,' Sir Francis put in with flattering deference. 'The letters are so . . . so *bizarre* in their accusations that one hardly knows whether to take them seriously or not.'

Henry was mollified. 'I think that it is a sound principle to take poison-pen letters seriously however far removed from truth their allegations may be.'

North murmured agreement. 'Very wise, but the accusations in this case are more than usually wild. A member of this household—his identity is not more precisely specified—is accused of kidnapping and murdering two girls.'

Henry paused, his glass half way to his lips. 'But surely,

18

if two girls had been kidnapped, not to say murdered, there would have been publicity—at least locally.'

Sir Francis nodded. 'You would think so, certainly, but it is a fact that two girls have—well—disappeared in recent months; that is to say, they have left home and have not been heard of since. But both girls were of age, they have been at loggerheads with their parents for years and both packed suitcases with their belongings which they took with them.'

'They left at the same time?'

'No. Eileen Cassels went sometime in October and Gillian Ford towards the end of November—about a month ago. They were, however, close friends and it seems likely that the second girl went to join the first.'

'What were the attitudes of the parents?'

Sir Francis looked to North for support. 'I think you would agree, Gerald, that the parents were not in the least surprised?'

Gerald did agree. 'Their attitudes could be summed up as resentful but resigned.'

Lucy had not touched her food since the subject of the missing girls had been raised, she looked from one to another as though hanging on every word that was spoken. Susan was puzzled by her more than ordinary concern. Now Lucy burst out, 'Resentful! What right have they to feel resentful with the kind of home life they provided for their children? It's no wonder the girls cleared out as soon as they were of age and could support themselves. The marvel is that they didn't go before.'

Sir Francis smiled, rather offensively indulgent. 'Lucy knew both the girls well, she has been their unofficial foster mother for years.' He caught Susan's eye and seemed to enlist her in a conspiracy of ridicule. 'Lucy is much given to good works.'

Susan could not begin to weave the threads of relationship into any sort of pattern but she was increasingly aware of a general uneasiness that seemed to possess the house and its occupants, and of cross currents of antagonism inexplicable to a stranger.

Henry addressed himself to North. 'So that the only connec-

19

tion between the girls and *Peel* was Mrs. North's social work?'

Gerald was engaged in the meticulous sectioning of an orange but he looked up, 'Yes, that is so. It is true that the girls came here several times but so do others.'

Henry sipped his wine. 'How many of these letters have been received?'

North paused in the act of lifting a segment of orange to his mouth. 'Harold has had two I believe, including one which came this morning, I have had three and Francis three.'

'Over what period?'

Words came from North with scarcely any movement of his lips and certainly with no change of his expression. 'About a month. The first came, addressed to me, just two days after the second girl left home.'

'You have the letters?'

Gerald looked Henry straight in the eye. 'No, not all of them, at first we agreed to treat them with the contempt they deserved.'

Harold produced an envelope from his pocket. 'This is the one I received this morning.'

The inevitable cheap envelope and paper, the address and message printed in block capitals with a ball-point pen. In this instance the message read:

IT IS A WASTE OF TIME TO WRITE TO YOU SO I AM WRITING TO THE POLICE.

Henry read the message and handed it back. 'If he keeps his promise your dilemma will be resolved, the police will start asking questions.'

It was a bald statement, lacking in tact and it was followed by an awkward silence.

Back in the drawing-room for coffee and polite conversation; non-controversial now. Sir Francis on his best behaviour. Harold Vane soon excused himself and what little life there had been in the party seemed to go with him.

'*Endure fort*,' Sir Francis murmured as the door closed. 'The Vane family motto, somewhat punningly translated as *Bear bravely*. Poor Harold, he has enough to put up with but he

20

reminds you rather of a bear, don't you think? A pleasant domestic variety but, nevertheless, with a dangerous hug.'

Susan found her gaze wandering from Gerald to Lucy and back again. She was speculating on what happened in their conjugal bed. There were no children at any rate. She caught Henry's eye and knew that he had read her thoughts.

The evening wore on until at half past ten Henry felt able to plead a long day and they broke up.

Susan went to her room; somebody had turned down the bed and laid out her nightdress. Lucy? There seemed to be no servants other than the paradoxical Flossie and a day girl. What would Lucy make of transparent nylon? She undressed; the central heating kept the room almost too warm and she went to the window. Standing in front of the blue velvet drapes she was cut off from the room, more a part of the night outside. The rain had cleared and a threequarter moon rode high in a broad rift of the clouds, its light refracted strangely in the bevelled glass of the window panes. She was looking down on the white steps and the balustrade with the park beyond. The distant fringe of trees seemed mysterious, menacing. A city girl, woods had for her a certain fearful romanticism no doubt attributable to the inclusion in her childhood literary diet of Grimm and various Transylvanian romances. As she watched she saw a figure moving across the grass away from the house, walking swiftly, almost trotting, it soon disappeared in the trees. Johnny Vane the idiot boy; no mistaking his unnatural bulk. She was so absorbed that a tap on her door and the noise of the catch startled her. It was Henry, in his dressing-gown.

'Well?' She picked up her own dressing-gown from the bed and slipped it on.

He shrugged. 'I don't think we shall spend Christmas playing *Happy Families*, do you?' He put his arm round her and drew her to him but she twisted away with impatience.

'Sorry!'

'It's not that. It's just that I don't like being petted absent-mindedly like a tame cat.'

'Is that what you think it is?'

He looked at her, a flicker of a smile on his lips. 'How old are you, Susan?'

'Twenty-four—why?'

'I should lock your door. There seems to be somebody about with an unhealthy interest in attractive young women.' With his hand on the door knob he paused and turned back to her. 'Good night!' He was gone.

'Bastard!' Susan said without heat.

She drew back the heavy curtains and went to bed but she did not lock her door.

CHAPTER TWO

A CLEAR, CRISP, cold morning, a faded blue sky. 'A weak ridge of high pressure moving in from the Atlantic will give dry cold weather everywhere at first to be followed later . . .' Christmas Eve. Susan remembered Christmas Eves of her childhood, there seemed to be an infinitude of them, spanning great vistas of time. The excitement, scarcely to be contained. A trip to the West End shops, with her mother in the morning, the empty endless desert of the afternoon, then up West again in the evening, after dark, to see the lights; patterns of points of brilliant light on the retina, painfully sharp against the velvet sky. Her father's hand, warm and immense. It never rained. Back home on a crowded, brightly lit bus, then supper and bed with the delicious expectation of presents in the morning. But little girls grow to become young women and their ideas change.

Henry was to spend the morning with Sir Francis being briefed for his task in the library so she was free. He would only need her when the real work of cataloguing began. She offered to help with the housework but although Lucy was profuse in her thanks she seemed unable to suggest anything that Susan could do, so she put on her duffle coat and set off to see something of the estate. She crossed the park, which was bigger than it looked, the few cows grazing paid her no attention, and she entered the trees. They were pines, and a neat little board by the path told her that this was the *Pinetum*, that it occupied more than twenty-five acres, that there were seventy species and nearly a thousand trees. H.R.H. The Prince of Wales planted one during his stay at *Peel* in 1883 but it did not say which and no prize was offered. Evidently *Peel Place* was opened to the public from time to time, either for charity or to help pay the bills.

It was a real wood but too conscientiously docketed for Susan's liking. You feel rather too secure from wolves, bears and wild boars as well as from most other hazards in a clump of *Abies pectinata* (European Silver Fir) each with a little metal name badge on its trunk. The ground climbed steeply to a ridge and then dropped away more slowly, the trees thinned and gave place to massive clumps of rhododendron between which Susan followed a path encouraged by little arrowed signs, *To the Willow Garden*. It was quite warm in the sun.

Then she exclaimed in surprise and pleasure. Oxford Street and the lights over again. The rhododendrons were left behind and she was standing on the edge of a broad shallow basin, a screen of trees round the rim but grassy slopes running down to an extensive lake, and there were houses with overhanging eaves and red-tiled roofs swept up at the corners in an absurd flourish—Chinese houses. There was a bridge too, and an island. A stage set for the Willow Pattern story but it was not a stage set, it was real.

'Mad, isn't it?'

She was startled. The voice came from behind her and she had heard no one. A youngish man in dirty corduroy slacks and a polo-necked jersey, stocky, with a great mop of unruly black hair, a ready smile showing good teeth and a vague resemblance she couldn't place.

'But all the Leighs are mad.'

Susan, at a loss for something to say, said nothing.

'This was one of the particular follies of great-great-great-grandfather Joseph Leigh, the second owner of *Peel Place* after they booted the Vanes out. Born 1749, departed this life in the fear of the Lord 1828. He had good reason to fear the Lord, by all accounts, having seduced or raped everything approximately eligible within a radius of ten miles. They bedded him down in the church finally under half a ton of masonry to keep him there. If you don't believe it, you can go and see for yourself. I'm Edward Leigh, by the way, who are you?'

Susan told him. 'You live on the estate?'

He looked at her with a curious expression. He seemed amused by her. 'You could say that but it would be nearer the truth to say that my brother's benevolence enables me to maintain a precarious existence in a former gamekeeper's cottage.'

'Don't you do any work?'

'I'm a painter.'

'Houses or canvas?'

'Hardboard, as a matter of fact, it's cheaper.'

'Do you manage to sell your paintings?'

'My dear child! I told you, I'm a painter. Artists may sell their daubs to a gullible and undiscriminating public but painters—never! They are always fifty years ahead of their times and their genius is unrecognized. Their work accumulates in dusty attics and or damp cellars until the rest catch up. The painter is then dead but his genius is discovered, to live on providing gilt-edged investment for poxy property tycoons and fat emasculated oil men. Didn't your mother ever tell you anything?'

'What do you paint?'

'Nudes mostly. The trouble is that they are a little too—abstruse—to sell to dirty old men and if they weren't they would be banned as grossly obscene. Do you follow?'

'I'm doing my best.'

They walked together down the grassy slope toward the lake and stood by the elaborate stone balustrade which surrounded the Pavilion and the Mandarin's house. 'It makes you think, doesn't it?'

24

'The art racket?'

'No, this. Imagine it: the mentality of a kid playing with his box of bricks, employing a hundred or so men for a couple of years in the process. And all because he was stupid enough to want to give life to a phoney legend based on the pattern of a dinner plate! There's wealth for you!'

'Nowadays he would have to pay it over in taxation to provide somebody else's kids with free milk or school dinners or to build a hundred yards of motor road. Does that suit you better?'

He looked at her with a certain fierceness, then he laughed. 'By God, it does! I lull myself to sleep gloating over the buggers who pay sur-tax and death duties.'

'Are you a Comrade?'

'How did you guess?'

'Can we go in?'

'In there?' He pointed to the Pavilion. 'Of course! Coach loads of the proletariat tramp all over the place in the summer at three bob a time, half a crown extra for a sampan on the lake and another three bob if you want tea in the Pavilion.'

The Pavilion was an outsized gazebo, octagonal in shape with five of its sides closed in and the other three open through lacquered pillars. Inside it was a disappointment, the red-tiled floor littered with dry and dusty leaves blown in by the wind, two stacks of folding tables, a quantity of stacking chairs, a counter with some veiled tea-making device and a group of large bottled-gas containers ranged against one wall, looking lethal. There was a telephone in a glass-fronted wall cupboard.

'Look.' He pointed to a lengthy inscription on two of the wall sections, done in faded gilt on red lacquer:

There was a great house belonging to a powerful Mandarin . . .

The Pavilion opened to the lakeside where there was a wooden staging and the bridge. Drawn up on the staging, out of the water, were ten or a dozen little flat-bottomed boats bearing a sketchy resemblance to sampans though much smaller. The inevitable white-on-green notice:

Half an hour 2/6d. Children must be accompanied by an adult.
Visitors hiring boats do so at their own risk.

Susan was disenchanted. But the willow *(Salix Babylonica)* was impressive, leafless now but in summer it must have rivalled the great trees that trail their weeping branches in the Cherwell. Although the sun still shone, Susan shivered.

'Cold?'

'I don't know. This place is vaguely depressing.'

'It's that bloody tree. I'm superstitious about willows; if I had my way I'd give it the chop but it's good for business. Come and see the Mandarin's house.'

The Mandarin's house was two storeys high *to show rank and wealth of its possessor* but the second storey was a fake and the house really consisted of three large intercommunicating rooms on the ground floor. Whether it had ever borne any resemblance to the interior of an eighteenth century Chinese gentleman's house Susan did not know but it seemed unlikely. Now it was a museum of local history or a means of extracting yet another shilling from the suckers, depending on your point of view. Susan was giving cursory attention to an exhibit of kitchen utensils through the ages.

'You've got a good figure.'

'Thanks.'

'Come along after lunch to my cottage and I'll go into details.'

'I shall be working. Are you married?'

'No, but I've got a nice line in double-beds. But listen, talking of your employer, which we weren't, isn't he connected with the police or something?'

'Or something. He's a zoologist but he has dabbled in criminology, if that's what you mean. His name has been in the paper in connection with one or two cases.'

'I thought so. Memory like an elephant. I suppose you realize that he's here about the girls?'

26

'What girls?'

'The missing girls, you must have heard something?'

'Your brother mentioned them last night.'

'I'll bet he did!'

'But they are nothing to do with Dr. Pym's visit. He is cataloguing the natural history material in the library.'

Edward picked up a rather complex mid-nineteenth century grid-iron and examined her through its convolutions. 'I wonder who thought of that?'

'The invitation came from Sir Francis.'

'It would, but dear Frankie never thought up that one, it's far too simple, and credible. Frankie would have tried something more ingenious and unlikely; he has a devious mind.'

'Are you suggesting that Dr. Pym was brought down here to investigate the disappearance of these girls? It's . . .'

Edward tipped the grid-iron forward until it just touched the tip of her nose. 'I'm not suggesting anything, little friend, I'm telling you that your bug hunter is here to find out who is writing nasty poison-pen letters. He may not know it yet, but it will emerge.'

Susan was becoming exasperated. 'But it's simply not possible—the invitation arrived a month ago—the twenty-fifth of November, to be precise . . .'

Edward smiled. 'The Ford girl left home on the twentieth and dear Gerald had his first letter on the twenty-second.'

'But it doesn't make sense! I mean, what . . . ?'

'You're very pretty. Your hair is the colour of ripe corn—not the stuff you get round here but as you see it in the fields of Provence—as van Gogh saw it. Ripened by the sun—a sun that eats into your soul and into your guts. Do you know Provence?'

'No—yes—what the hell has that got to do with it anyway?'

'Burnished gold—hackneyed—but apt in this case. And when you get pettish a faint flush just heightens the colour of those cheeks like a touch of rouge applied with exquisite skill.'

'I'm asking you what the disappearance of those girls can

27

possibly have to do with Sir Francis?'

'More than you think. There's been a lot of gossip in the town and round the countryside, and all the gossip leaves one of us here at *Peel* holding the dirty end—they're not fussy.'

'But why? Why should they pick on the Leighs?'

Edward had dropped the grid-iron and was now standing, examining her critically. 'I can't be quite sure about the breasts with that damn coat. Have you got good breasts?'

Susan had reached her limit. 'For God's sake stop fooling and try to talk sense for two minutes! If the police ever do begin looking for a sex maniac they won't have to look far.'

'Now you've hurt me. But to answer your question: the locals pick on us partly because Frankie has quite a reputation where young girls are concerned and partly because they believe that there is an historical precedent. Ancestor Joseph, God rest his soul, was as I told you much given to the sports of the bedchamber. Had he contented himself with the more or less orthodox repertoire of the lecher, he was wealthy enough to hush up any scandal. The odd defloration or pregnancy, even, need not have troubled him unduly. But it is said that as he got old he developed a taste for certain specialized variations which he dared not allow to be known and so he is accused of kidnapping girls who never returned to their fond mammas again. Nine of them.'

'You mean that he killed nine girls?'

'So it was said though never proved. The Leighs have never done things by halves. However, the story goes that he died just in time, an aggrieved body of the peasantry arrived one night with the declared intention of burning the place down about his ears and were only appeased when his son, Roger, a democratically-minded cove, admitted them to view his father's corpse.'

Susan was both shocked and puzzled. 'But that was a hundred and fifty years ago! I mean, people wouldn't think of it now—they wouldn't even *know*.'

Edward smiled, the smile that was beginning to infuriate

28

her. 'How right you are! Such percipience! Somebody, my child, with mischievous intent, has been stirring the ancient slime. A whispering campaign and anonymous letters. My dear brother and Gerald are really quite worried. Can you wonder that they should try to enlist the aid of your clever bug hunter? Gerald is behind it, of course. "Get this man down here, Francis, on this or that pretext, then play it by ear." Gerald is a great fixer.'

'I must be getting back,' Susan said.

'Walk back with me to the cottage and I'll run you home in the car.'

They crossed the lake by the bridge and came to an estate road which climbed the opposite slope through trees and took them in a quarter of a mile of walking to Edward's cottage. Four square, stone built, but nestling comfortably into a gentle slope backed by trees with a walled garden in front. A newish Mini parked by the gate suggested some reward for the painter or a burst of brotherly benevolence.

'Come in and see my etchings.'

'Another time.'

Just then Johnny Vane came out of the trees and lolloped down the grassy slope to stand by the little car, grinning. Edward patted his shoulder. 'I promised him a ride. I taught him to drive but he's not allowed to drive off the estate and Francis won't let him drive on it unless there's somebody with him. But you're not so stupid as they think, are you, Johnny?'

Johnny nodded and widened his grin.

'He's a deaf mute. They say he's also mentally deficient and that's why he was never sent to a special school but that's a load of crap. Johnny's got it but he's never been allowed to use it.' Susan was surprised by the gentle expressiveness of Edward's features whenever he looked at Johnny, and the boy never took his eyes off him.

'Do you object to Johnny as a chauffeur?'

They drove back, Susan beside the driver, Edward in the back seat.

'The joker who's rattling the family skeleton has had a

29

go at Johnny too. He is careful to point out that the notorious Joseph had a deaf mute as his personal servant, a giant negro called Jeremiah. According to the story it was he who kidnapped the girls for the old boy.'

Meanwhile Johnny drove the car at a sedate pace, changing gear with faultless precision, his features set in a smile of unalloyed bliss.

'You and I will be seeing a lot of each other,' Edward prophesied as they parted.

Gerald did not come home for lunch but there were two newcomers, Beth Vane, Harold's daughter, Johnny's sister, and a pretty Chinese girl whom they called Mei Mei. Beth Vane, stocky like her father and good-looking in a no nonsense sort of way, had a mop of fair hair and boundless enthusiasm, neither of which was very well controlled. 'We're in the middle of dressing the Christmas tree,' she told Susan. 'Mei Mei is marvellous, she can do anything with a few bits of tinsel and wire.'

'Not true!' Mei Mei said, smiling modestly and folding her hands in her lap.

'Anyway, you'll see tonight,' Beth promised. 'But the drawing-room is out of bounds until then. Understand everybody?' Then she added as an afterthought, 'If that's all right with you, Uncle Francis?'

Sir Francis was at his most genial, and Henry, too, seemed in good humour.

'An astonishing amount of most valuable material, Susan, some of it unique. This will be a rewarding task.'

'It is most kind of you to undertake it.' From Sir Francis. 'I scarcely hoped that I should be fortunate enough to interest you in my little project.'

'My dear Leigh! I assure you that the obligation is mine.'
Susan would have liked to make a rude noise.

'Your ancestor, Joseph Leigh, appears to have been a truly remarkable person, a man of quite exceptional talents,' Henry went on.

And how! Susan said, 'I've been hearing something of Joseph Leigh already this morning.'

30

'Indeed?' Polite but a little frosty.

'From your brother Edward.'

'Edward! If you heard anything from him it must have been something scandalous. He takes a mischievous delight in digging up family skeletons and in inventing them when the vaults are empty.' Sir Francis laughed at his own whimsy. 'A delightful personality; though as his brother, I shouldn't say so. But like all creative people Edward is slightly mad.'

CHAPTER THREE

THE SKY CLOUDED after lunch, a high impenetrable veil of grey, bleaching all colour from the landscape and seeming to intensify the cold. 'Snow tonight!' Henry said. They had to have the lights on in the library but it was warm there. The room occupied the whole of the ground floor of the new wing added after demolition of the mansion. But linen-fold panelling from the old library and a simple undecorated ceiling of plain beams and white plaster made it seem older than the rest of the house. The books were stored in double cases placed at right angles to the walls forming bays with a broad carpeted aisle down the middle. A great wooden chest covered with elaborately tooled leather stood in one of the bays, its lid raised, disclosing a shallow tray divided into sections most of them stuffed with envelopes tied into bundles with blue tape.

'Joseph's filing system. Sir Francis had it brought down here for our convenience.'

'Big of him,' Susan said.

Several bundles of envelopes had been removed and lay on the table, their tapes untied. Henry was like a boy stamp collector with a newly arrived packet of five thousand unsorted. 'Take your pick!'

Susan picked up an envelope from one of the piles and extracted a sheet of stiff paper, yellowed at the edges and along the folds:

Selborne August 1st. 1770.

Dear Sir,

I am much gratified by your letter from which I derive the more satisfaction on account of your living in the most westerly county where it may be anticipated that the courses of Nature run somewhat differently . . .

'Gilbert White!' Susan exclaimed. 'Are there any more of his?'

'Ten or a dozen and there are at least three from Moses Harris, one promising to send a copy of "my newly published work, the *Aurelian's Pocket Companion*".' Henry was positively gloating. 'I tell you, Susan, this may be a really important find. If the rest of the stuff is anything like this, it will make a significant contribution to the history of eighteenth-century science. It will also mean that Joseph Leigh was an interesting and important figure.'

'I saw some of Joseph's work this morning.'

'Indeed?'

'The Willow Garden.'

Henry sat back in his chair, his interest roused. 'Of course! I remember reading of it at one time as one of the features of *Peel* but I'd forgotten. You must take me there. Joseph was clearly a man of parts.'

'Yes. Among his other accomplishments he seems to have been a kidnapper and a murderer.' She told him the story as Edward had told it to her and he listened with attention but all he said was, 'So the present disappearances are being linked with an alleged precedent. Now that *is* interesting.'

With that mixture of anticipation and misgiving with which one lights the blue touch paper, Susan added, 'Edward also said that you have been brought here under false pretences, that Sir Francis intended from the first to involve you in the investigation.'

32

To Susan's astonishment, Henry accepted this without the slightest surprise or indignation. 'That is extremely probable. I suspected as much after our conversation last night.'

'And we are staying on?'

'Certainly! Why not? There is no pretence about the interest of these letters and if I can be of any assistance in the other matter, then so much the better. Relax, Susan! Enjoy yourself, it is the season of goodwill.'

Susan was impressed; she had rarely seen Henry so amenable to the designs of others. 'Do you really think that these girls have been kidnapped and that the Leighs may be involved?'

Henry frowned. 'Two singularly unprofitable questions. How can I possibly express an opinion on either?'

They settled down to a systematic exploration of the contents of the trunk, listing and classifying. The piles on the table grew and the entries in Susan's notebook multiplied. As they delved deeper the proportion of letters concerned with the phenomena of natural history decreased and there were more of a private nature, from relatives and friends, reflecting the lives of those who wrote them. It seemed that Joseph had a married sister who led a rather gay life in London and her letters were full of socialite gossip, often scandalous. She taunted him with the dreariness of his life at *Peel* and professed pity for the lot of his wife Caroline. *I do believe that you have more regard for your tiresome birds and insects than for your lovely wife and your little son.* But Caroline did not long remain a competitor for his interest, she died when their son Roger was five years old of a mysterious *flux of the bowels*. She was twenty-two.

After the second tray and the turn of the century, nearly all the letters, whether scientific or personal, were addressed to Roger, who seemed to take on precisely where his father left off, though Joseph was little more than fifty with nearly thirty years of life in front of him. On the evidence, Susan was ready to believe that he had discovered other, less creditable, interests.

'Like peeping through keyholes, isn't it?' Henry inter-

33

rupted her absorption in the letters. 'Or eavesdropping on other people's conversation.'

'I see no resemblance.'

Henry laughed. 'Be honest with yourself, Susan. The motivation is the same. We find it difficult to believe that others are as weak, as mean, as petty as ourselves, so we pry into their secret lives whenever we have the chance, looking for reassurance. Fortunately, we usually find it.'

'Fortunately?'

'Of course. Otherwise lunatic asylums would be fuller than they are.'

Sir Francis came in and stood at the end of the table. 'My word! This looks like progress. I hope that you won't be too efficient and deprive us of your company before we are better acquainted. We live rather dull and uneventful lives here and your visit is a milestone.' The lamplight glistened on his spectacles and his eyes seemed to dance with childish enthusiasm. Susan found herself aggravated afresh by his bonhomie though she could hardly have explained why. Sir Francis *looked* good-humoured and benevolent, he had the build for it, the countenance, a bouncing little man. But she could not believe in this version, nor was her disbelief due to the absurd reactionary views which he professed. She had to admit to a prejudice against sugar daddies and apart from what Edward had said it was too easy to see Sir Francis in that rôle.

'One of the estate people brought your car back and I had it put in No. 3 garage in the old stables at the rear of the house. I understand the malady has been cured.' He dropped the keys on the table.

Henry thanked him.

'And now, Lucy tells me that there is some tea in the dining-room. The drawing-room is still out of bounds.' He smiled and talked his way out.

'Nice fellow,' Henry remarked and Susan could not tell whether he intended to be provocative. 'We'd better go.'

'Let's lift out this last tray and see what's underneath.'

The bottom of the trunk was not divided into sections

34

as the trays had been. It contained only four large leather-bound books, lying flat, each with a gilt number on its cover. Susan picked up the first of them:

Being the Diary and Commonplace Book of Roger Leigh of Peel in the County of Cornwall

Together with Observations on Natural Phenomena for the Years 1790–1799

She turned the page.

'April 21st. 1790. Today, the fifth day of my being confined to my room of the Mumps, the swelling and soreness of the throat much decreased, I do begin to keep a diary . . .'

She consulted her notes. 'Precocious little blighter! He was fourteen when he wrote that.'

'They were hard times for youth,' Henry said. 'But let's go in to tea.'

Outside dusk intensified the gloom, slate grey clouds hung low like smoke over the park and at any moment one expected to see the first fluttering tentative snow flakes.

Beth Vane and the Chinese girl gave them tea.

'Mei Mei is training to be a nurse at the hospital. Daddy was a great friend of her family when he was in Malaya so now she lives with us.'

Susan wondered about Mummy.

'I shall go back to Malaysia when I am qualified,' Mei Mei said in case her patriotism was in question.

'If you don't marry an English boy before then which is extremely likely.'

'Not true!' Mei Mei sat bolt upright on her chair, her features composed, a model of Victorian rectitude, an effect that was almost immediately spoiled by an irrepressible chuckle. 'But it is still untrue what Beth says,' she added.

'The party begins at seven, supper at nine and at midnight —well, you'll have to wait and see.' Beth was young for her age and what her grandmother would have called a *Tomboy*, probably because she was spoiled.

'This thing tonight,' Henry said, when they were alone. 'They will probably be giving presents. We ought to have thought . . .'

'I did. I bought a variety of useful and seasonable gifts. At least, that's what the shop called them.'

'Bless you! You think of everything.'

'I'll get you to put that in writing. But you'd better come along to my room before the fun starts to decided who is to have what.'

In fact the things which Susan had bought were still in a suitcase in the boot of the car and she decided to fetch them before it became really dark. The inevitable green baize door which she had not previously passed through led into a stone passage and then to strip lighting, plastic tiles, formica surfaces, eye-level cupboards, a smell of mince-pies, and Flossie.

'You wanted something, Miss?' Flossie was distinctly unwelcoming.

'The garage,' Susan said. 'I want to get something from the car.'

Flossie seemed inexplicably relieved. 'I'll put on the outside lights. Yours is the third garage from the left. There's a wicket and, inside, a switch on the wall to the right. I'll give you a torch.'

Such solicitude made Susan wonder what the old girl imagined she had come for in the first place. She crossed a brightly lit cobbled yard. The air was still and cold and filled with feathery flakes that vanished as they drifted to the ground. She found the garage and as she pushed open the wicket she thought she heard a scuffle inside. She explored the darkness with the beam of her torch. 'Is anyone there?'

Silence. Perhaps there were rats. A big place with plenty of room for another car. The floor was cobbled and the partitions were of varnished wood, they stopped at about six feet and they did not reach the full length so that it was possible to pass from one garage to the next. Susan felt nervous but she found the switch and the brilliant cold strip lighting was reassuring. Almost at once she noticed that the front number plate was badly buckled and a closer look showed that the bumper was dented. The estate people or the garage? She would have to tread warily. She inspected the car all round but there was no other damage. She was about to open the boot when it occurred to her that she had not recorded the mileage of their trip to *Peel*. Despite Henry's ridicule she had kept a note of every trip and of all petrol and oil used since the car was new. She got into the driving seat, took the log book from the glove tray and entered the reading. They had clocked fifty-seven miles since leaving Gurnick the previous morning. Fifty-seven miles! At a generous estimate it was no more than twenty-one. Allow three miles into town and back, a possible couple of miles for a road test and somebody had still driven twenty-eight unauthorized miles. She switched on the ignition. The petrol gauge showed a quarter full but it had been rather more than half full when they left Gurnick—say three and a half gallons, and that checked with the recorded mileage.

Johnny? But he could hardly have had access to the keys. Which left a garage hand or one of the estate men. She was annoyed but she knew that Henry would object to any fuss. She got out of the car, but before closing the door, she swept the interior with the beam of her torch, looking for oil or grease stains. Nothing of the sort. The upholstery was immaculate. She was about to slam the door when her attention was caught by a thin metallic gleam from the crevice between the back of the passenger seat and the seat itself. She reached in and probed with her fingers. A gold chain with a cross. Not only an excuse but an obligation to find out a bit more about the offenders. Susan smiled. She disliked unsolved mysteries.

At that moment she heard the noise again. No rat. There was somebody in the garage next door. Without giving herself time to think she made for the gap in the partition at the back but before she reached it, Edward came through, blinking in the light.

'I thought you must have settled down for the night. What the hell were you doing?'

She was indignant. 'More to the point, what were you doing, skulking in the dark?'

He smiled. 'A fair question. I didn't particularly want to to be seen and I was waiting for you to go.'

'But surely you could have got out through the wicket in the other door.'

He shook his head. 'The car next door is Gerald's and he locks the bloody thing in. He's the sort to lock his bloody braces for fear somebody tries to pinch his pants.'

'You still haven't said what you were doing.'

'I might ask what the hell it's got to do with you but instead I'll content myself with—no comment!'

'But you still don't want Gerald to know you were here.'

'Exactly.' He was grinning at her but she had the impression that he was concerned.

'You weren't by any chance, looking for this?' She held up the chain.

The grin vanished. 'Could be. Where did you find it?'

'Whose is it?'

'I haven't a clue.'

'I found it down the back of the passenger seat, here.'

'Well I'm damned!'

'Was it you who used the car for a joy ride?'

'I wouldn't ride in that bloody hearse if you paid me. I like something with a bit more dash. But what's this about a joy ride?'

Susan told him and he looked serious. 'Twenty-eight miles.' He was silent for a time, then he demanded, 'Are you going to show that cross to your bug hunter?'

'Of course.'

He nodded. 'You do that. But if you value our maturing friendship my child, you won't mention me.'

'I'll think about it.'

He shivered. 'Christ! It's cold. If I stay here much longer I shall join the brass monkeys.'

38

'That might not be a bad thing.'

He put his arm round her. 'You're a bloody sadist but I think I could live with you.'

As they were crossing the yard, he said, 'I suppose you realize that I could have slugged you, raped you and left you lying on those cold hard cobbles?'

'The thought had crossed my mind.'

'Then don't be such a bloody fool again. I might next time.'

She had forgotten the presents and they had to go back for them. The yard was white with snow and they made crisp incisive footprints.

He left her at the back door. 'I'm off! See you later.'

CHAPTER FOUR

WHEN HENRY CAME to her room to sort out the presents, Susan showed him the cross and told him about the car. He took it more seriously than she had expected. 'Twenty-eight miles. Of course, it could be a chap from the estate showing off to his girl-friend. But what about Edward—do you think he was going over our car before you arrived?'

It was the question uppermost in her own mind. 'I don't know. I suppose I made enough noise crossing the yard to warn him if he was.'

'We'll take a closer look at the car in the morning.'

'Will you say anything to Sir Francis?'

He shook his head. 'Not at the moment.'

They allocated and labelled the presents and when he was leaving, Henry said, 'Edward has probably fallen for you, but don't take any chances!'

'He really does think there's something wrong here . . . or else . . .' You could never tell with Henry.

But twenty minutes later she was feeling proud to be with him as they walked down the staircase together. His dark suit set off the extreme pallor of his features, his innate dignity enabled him to carry off his height and his lean, almost emaciated figure. He was made for walking down broad carpeted stairs with an elegant and beautiful woman on his arm. To greet with condescending charm little groups of admiring and aspiring mortals gathered to pay their humble respects. Usually that was what she most disliked about him. But there were no such groups tonight. In fact there was nobody until they pushed open the door of the drawing-room, where there seemed to be everybody, and everybody talking at once.

The girls had done their work well. A huge Christmas tree *(Picea excelsis)* dominated the space in front of the windows, draped with lights and richly coloured glass balls. Tinsel glistened and elaborate paper chains with an eastern motif swept in graceful curves from the chandelier to the four corners. Not forgetting the holly *(Ilex aquifolium)*. The only light came from the tree, from Chinese lanterns hung on the chains and from the fire, made up with logs.

Sir Francis came forward, a little flushed. 'Come over to the fire. Let me see now, is there anyone you don't know? Helen! Of course, you haven't met Helen.'

Talking of elegant and beautiful women! Helen Vane in green figured taffeta, high necked, chaste. Grecian features surmounted by golden hair in coiled plaits like a diadem. Hera, a trifle soured by her husband's infidelities. But scarcely old enough to be mother to Johnny and Beth. Puzzling. To Susan she was coldly polite. Hardly more forthcoming to Henry, though Susan noticed that he got a second, longer look. What was farmer Harold doing with this bird of paradise? And what did she do to him? Susan wished that she had worn something a bit more competitive.

Mei Mei in a cheong sam of flame-coloured silk was eye-catching too. Breathtaking.

Lucy and Beth were their foils, homely, not to say dowdy. Susan was grateful. Edward had made himself conspicuous by wearing tight black trousers and a finely knitted black polo-necked jersey like a cat burglar. He winked, taking his attention momentarily off Mei Mei with whom he was engaged in animated conversation. 'I hope she knows how to look after herself,' Susan thought. 'He ought to be chained up or labelled or just neutered.'

Gerald North talked to Harold Vane. They typified *The Law* and *The Land*, almost cartoon figures from *Punch*. Gerald, parchment features, thin lipped, introspective and dyspeptic. Harold, bluff, friendly, apparently full of animal spirits. Animal spirits—was that what Helen got out of it? The classic mould sometimes hides strange potentialities. Susan knew a girl of Helen's stamp who insisted on her bull mastiff sharing the bath with her.

Sir Francis stood in front of the fire and gathered their attention. 'It is past seven and, as most of you know, it has become a tradition to start our Christmas Eve party with one of Lucy's Treasure Hunts, and that is what we shall do tonight.' He might have been a vicar opening a bazaar. 'Lucy!'

Lucy came into the firelight, a tiny wad of typewritten papers in her hand. It took Susan a moment to place the image she recalled. An earnest, harassed little R.E. mistress, *Now Girls! Today we shall* . . . '. . . the first clue which I shall pass round in a moment. There are ten clues altogether and ten copies of each except the last. When you discover the second clue you should remove one of the copies and take it with you, and so on until you are led to the final one which you must bring to me here, along with the others. There is as usual a prize for the first home with a complete set of clues arranged in the correct order.' Her face showed animation for the first time; she looked at Edward with a slight smile. 'Obviously, if the game is to succeed, it is necessary to hunt alone rather than in pairs or in groups.'

Edward made some remark but it was lost in the general laughter.

'The hunt covers the whole house but there are no clues outside, this year.' She distributed her little bits of paper. 'I'm afraid it will be more difficult for you as you do not know the house very well . . .'

Susan read the clue.

> *Not any golden treasure,*
> *Nor any tyrant's pleasure*
> *May recall my measure.*
> *But search above and you may learn*
> *Those very facts for which you yearn.*

'You can't recall time,' Helen said.

'Sh!' From several. 'Don't give it away.'

One by one they took themselves off, self-conscious because they were playing children's games again but determined not to be shown up by the others. Susan was the last to leave and she picked up her torch from the table by the door. 'It will be more fun by torchlight,' Lucy had said. 'And in any case, you may not be able to find the light switches.'

No one in the hall but she could hear voices and see a complex of torch beams on the next floor. Certainly the clue suggested time and the invitation to search above seemed to mean upstairs. A clock upstairs. But wasn't this too obvious? If the whole competition was like that they would be falling over one another. She gave Lucy credit for more subtlety. What else was measured which could not be re-called? Material was sold by the yard, but that didn't make sense. Water? Milk? Surely you could recall them, whatever that meant. Gas? There didn't seem to be any in the house. *Electricity!* That must be it—she was looking for the electri-city meters. And they would be in or near the kitchen, perhaps in the cellar if there was one. She hoped not.

To her surprise, no light in the kitchen where Flossie should have been preparing the meal. But a reassuring warm fruity smell. A click and a tiny bulb lit up as the thermostat switched the oven on. All under control. Three doors; she knew the one that led to the yard so she must try the other two. A larder, icy cold, but with a great floor-to-ceiling refrigerator all the same. No meters. The second door opened into a broom cupboard big enough to be called a room. No meters to be seen so she stepped into the room and closed the door behind her to see if they were hidden by it. The figure of a man standing there made her jump. 'I'm sorry. My torch has gone wrong.' Gerald North fiddling with his torch by a wall cupboard containing a selection of fuse boxes and two meters. 'We seem to have had the same idea, but there is nothing here.'

'Have you tried the top of the cupboard? It says, search above.'

She held her torch beam steady while he ran his hand across the top of the cupboard. 'Ah! You are right! Dear me! Lucy might have dusted it first.' He removed one of the flimsy papers handed it to her and put the others back under a reel of fuse wire.

'Don't you want one?'

She couldn't see his face but his voice was dry. 'I had already discovered the hiding place when you arrived but I was hoping to throw you off the scent. When I play, I play to win, I am rather a ruthless person.'

'Then you'd better go ahead and keep your advantage, hadn't you?'

He switched on his torch, which worked perfectly and stalked out.

The second clue took her to the attics. The whole house seemed to be in darkness save for the torch beams probing anonymously. Surprisingly quiet. Footsteps, an occasional scuffle, a sharp exclamation, whispering now and then, but none of the boisterous slightly hysterical nonsense she had expected. They took their treasure hunting seriously. Like Gerald, the old bastard! She climbed the stairs to the attics. They were narrow but carpeted. Perhaps Flossie slept up here. The torch showed a long passage with three doors on one side and two on the other. The first was locked but the second door opened. She had a glimpse of an uncurtained window and a collection of lumber, then a voice said, 'Christ, you've taken long enough, I thought you were brighter than that! Gerald and your bug hunter have been here already. Here! It's your next clue—from in that abortion on the mantelpiece.' He pointed with his torch. A Victorian vase in the form of a fish standing on its tail. *'Where Jonah lived three nights and days . . . I thought it was a bloody whale anyway.'*

'According to the Bible it was a great fish. But what are you doing here?'

'Waiting for you. Did you tell him?'

'Did I tell who what?'

He went over to the door, turned the key in the lock and switched on the light. 'Did you tell Pym about the car and the cross?'

'Yes.'

'And about me?'

'That too.'

'Oh. What's he going to do? Has he told Frankie?'

'I've no idea what he's going to do. *Were* you searching our car?'

He looked at her grinning. 'No. But I would have if I'd thought of it.'

Somebody tried the door. He put his arms round her, holding her tight. 'Keep quiet and they'll go away.'

'They'll see the light.'

'These doors are damn near airtight.'

After two or three attempts whoever it was moved off down the passage.

'There!' He let her go. 'Do you sleep with Pym?'

'No!'

'Then come back with me tonight.'

'No.'

'All right, I'll stay with you.'

'You will not!'

'It's a criminal waste.'

'You're obsessed!'

'Dedicated is the word.'

She switched off the light, unlocked the door cautiously and went out into the passage, leaving him there.

Twenty minutes later the hunt was still on and Susan had reached the eighth clue. She had come across most of the competitors and one supernumerary. Coming down the main stairs her torch beam fell on Johnny, standing in the angle on the first landing. He was grinning. He had on a navy blue mackintosh which looked very wet and there were snow flakes in his hair. At the bottom of the stairs she met Lucy and told her.

'Oh, Johnny's all right. He wanders around; it's hopeless to try to keep him in one place.'

> *Mightier than the sword,*
> *Its armoury enshrines the clue.*
> *No more than half the letters through*
> *Truth is a stranger word.*
> *The fourth in line*
> *Page fifty nine.*

Susan had had trouble with this one. Now she had reached a conclusion. The pen is mightier than the sword and the armoury of the pen must mean the library. Half the letters through could be *M* and as truth is said to be stranger than fiction, she was hoping to find what she wanted on page fifty nine of the fourth book under *M* in the fiction section. The library was in darkness like the rest of the house but she pushed open the double doors and walked down the centre aisle with a greater confidence, she knew the ground and fiction was at the far end. The whole of the end wall and the two bays facing. She found *M* and counted along. Rose Macaulay's *Told by an Idiot*. Between pages fifty-nine and sixty there were several of the thin slips—she counted seven still there so she wasn't doing so badly. She took one, put the book back and then she heard a movement further down the room, a shuffle of feet on the wooden floor of one of the bays, quick footsteps on the carpet, then the click of the doors closing. Odd. There must have been someone there when she came in. She walked back down the aisle with no clear intention, then it occurred to her to look in the bay where she and Henry had been working. Everything was as they had left it except that one of Roger's diaries was open on the table. She was about to close it and replace it in the trunk when she noticed that pages had been removed —cleanly cut from the binding, leaving strips of paper less than a quarter of an inch wide. She looked at the dates. It was not the volume she had examined; it was the third volume, covering the years 1814–1830 and the missing pages —four of them—were taken from the year 1828, the middle of September as nearly as she could make out. Of course it was possible that the pages might have been removed at any time in the past hundred and forty years but she didn't think so. For one thing it would have been a coincidence that the book should lie open at that point and for another she thought that the adjacent pages were lying awkwardly, as though in an unaccustomed relationship. Odd. And annoying because she had already developed a sense of property in the contents of the trunk. But there was nothing she could do now. She put the mutilated book back in its place and made for the door but as she reached it the booming of the gong sounded the end of the hunt. Somebody had produced all the clues.

It was Gerald. Gerald had won for the past six years and good-humoured teasing had become as much a part of the tradition as the game itself. 'Prizes at the end of the party as usual,' Lucy announced. 'Supper now.'

A cold buffet in the dining-room. Chicken, ham, pork and tongue with a selection of attractive salad dishes and hot mince pies to follow. Everybody regretting the absence of a third hand or at least of a prehensile foot. Gerald had taken possession of one of the two small tables and invited Susan to share. He did not touch the meat and drank milk instead of wine.

'And how is the work going? Anything of interest?'

'Dr. Pym seems to think so. Scientifically speaking, it is a most interesting and valuable correspondence.'

'And otherwise?' He raised his thin eyebrows and regarded Susan with a smile she could not interpret.

'Otherwise? I don't understand.'

'Anything of interest from other points of view—family

history, for example?'

Susan laughed. 'I'm afraid that is outside our brief.'

'You are a very discreet young lady.' He sipped his milk and patted his lips with a paper table napkin. 'The Leighs are a strange family; they have had more than their share of eccentrics.'

'In any case, I imagine that someone has been through all the material before it was passed on to us.'

Gerald shook his head. 'I doubt it. I very much doubt it. It would be unlike Francis to do anything of the sort and I have never been given the opportunity.' A suggestion of pique? Susan thought so.

Henry seemed set on making himself pleasant to Lucy. They sat nearby, Henry juggling expertly with his plate and glass; Lucy held a plate of salad but she ate little. Susan tried to overhear their conversation while keeping her end up with Gerald North and she was pretty sure that he was doing the same. His wife was saying:

'But surely, Dr. Pym, some families have an inherited taint just as others have an inherited genius? The Galtons, the Darwins, the Huxleys must have their ill-starred counterparts.'

Susan, for the second time in a short acquaintance, was surprised by Lucy's fluency and by the implications of scholarship. Gerald seemed to divine her thoughts or perhaps he was developing his own theme: 'All the Leighs are abnormally intelligent. Lucy was up at Somerville and took a first in history. That surprises you, doesn't it? But there is always something which seems to frustrate their genius, something which stops it being successfully channelled into creative work. Look at Edward.' He shrugged. 'And Lucy contents herself with the housework.' He spoke in a low voice so that he would not be overheard but there was little risk for Henry was at full spate in the rôle of a distinguished scholar with his favourite pupil.

'I doubt if what you say is true in the sense in which you mean it. Obviously physical and mental attributes are handed on from one generation to the next. Some are desirable, others—not, but our genetic endowment is no more than a legacy of potentialities. What we achieve in our becoming is as much a matter of environment as of inheritance. Nurture and nature are equal partners in building the definitive personality.'

But Lucy was unimpressed. 'That seems to me a way of saying that although the process may be a more subtle one, the result is the same.'

'Not at all. You used the word "taint" which in its context is almost synonymous with bad blood. This is the language of superstition, not of science, and the ideas to which the words give expression are as unscientific as the words themselves.'

'I expect that you are right, at least that your theory is sound but in practice, the risks are too great.'

'Risks? Risks to whom?'

Her voice was hard. 'To a possible son or daughter.'

Susan caught Gerald's eye upon her and she blushed.

'Open it, Gerald!' Helen demanded. She stood over him, her beautiful features transformed out of their customary peevishness by excitement.

Gerald held a thin, square parcel wrapped in Christmas paper, his prize for winning the treasure hunt; he looked embarrassed. 'I think I know what is in it. Lucy relies on me winning her competition to keep me in handkerchiefs for another year.'

Helen had had too much to drink, she was flushed, her voice was too loud and all her movements were exaggerated. Susan wondered why it is more embarrassing to see a woman making a fool of herself than a man.

'Gerald, I insist!'

Harold Vane alone seemed totally unaware of any strain, he sat watching his wife with a tolerant smile but Beth was acutely embarrassed. She put her arm round Helen's shoulders and tried to lead her off. 'Come and sit with us, Helen; Mei Mei wants to show you the present she had from Uncle Francis.'

48

So Helen was not a marvel of youth preserved, not the mother of Beth and Johnny.

But she was at the critical stage in the drunk's progress. To be merry and amenable or morose and nasty. Unwittingly, Beth seemed to turn the scale. The foolish animation vanished and her face became hard. 'Blast Uncle Francis and his bloody presents! And get off my back, you stupid little bitch!' She snatched at the box, the immediate cause of the trouble and ripped off the decorated paper. Then she opened it and looked inside. She slumped heavily in her chair and stared into the box where the handkerchiefs should have been. 'There's nothing in it! Only paper!' She looked at Lucy and understanding grew in her eyes. 'Is this one of your little economies, Lucy? Giving an empty bloody box as a prize?' She laughed hysterically. 'You'd have looked bloody silly if anybody else won it—or were you quite sure that couldn't happen?'

Even Harold was stirred. He came over and took her firmly but kindly by the arm. 'Come on, my girl. Bed for you.' She followed him out of the room like a child. At the door, he turned back, 'We'll say goodnight. Thank you, Lucy, for a nice evening. Perhaps you'll bring Mei Mei and Beth home, Edward?'

Nobody said a word after the door closed behind them. Gerald sat looking at his box, holding in his hand some sheets of manuscript which Susan recognized at once.

CHAPTER FIVE

TWO FIFTEEN BY the clock on the bedside table, the house quiet as death, and all around the snow, a carpet of silence. Miles away a train rattled over the viaduct which spans the town. Christmas Day.

Susan sat on the rug by the electric fire and waited, wishing she had never come to *Peel*. The despondency of the

49

small hours and a seasonable nostalgia, the memory of other Christmases freed of all stress and frustration by the filtering process of time. A gentle tap on the door. Henry, still fully dressed, looking weary.

'Well? What did Sir Francis have to say?' Susan tried to sound brisk, God knows why.

He came into the room, slumped down in the armchair and handed her the small wad of manuscript papers. 'No progress. He simply gave me these and said he was glad I was in the house. He's a very worried man but he's not prepared to talk—yet. He made one odd remark though— "I feel that with you here, I've got a fair chance." ' Henry held out his thin white hands to the fire, he seemed to be chilled through. 'Flattering but hardly helpful. I asked him what he meant, whether he believed himself to be in danger. All he said was, "There's something very odd going on here, it's been building up for some time. As to danger, I don't expect to get a knife in the back or poison in my soup but there are other more subtle threats." I couldn't get any more.'

Two o'clock in the morning isn't the time for mysteries and Susan felt out of sympathy with the inhabitants of *Peel* and their bizarre affairs but Henry wriggled into a more relaxed position, his legs stretched out.

'Edward told you that somebody was trying to link the disappearance of these girls with Joseph's eccentricities and it looks as though there is someone in the house with the same idea. Perhaps we shall know better when we've read the cut-out pages. I don't suppose they were taken at random.'

Susan sat staring into the fire, one side of her face illuminated by its orange glow, burnishing her hair, the other in shadow. 'Whoever cut out those pages took a considerable risk of being caught in the act. If I'd been a few minutes sooner . . . I mean, they couldn't have worked by torchlight, could they? Selecting the passages and cutting them out—quite carefully—must have taken some time.'

Henry brushed the idea aside. 'They were cut out earlier, probably before we came to *Peel*. The chap you heard in the bay was putting his handiwork on show so that it wouldn't
50

be missed. I must have been there just a few minutes before you and there was nobody in the bay then and nothing on the table. I looked to make sure that we hadn't left any of our stuff lying about.' He broke off suddenly, looking down at her. 'Are you tired?'

Susan yawned. 'Dog tired but I'll read the stuff if you want me to?'

She sorted the pages and began to read, haltingly at first but with greater confidence as she became accustomed to the idiosyncrasies of the flowing script.

September 11th. Thursday.

Matters grow daily worse and I fear that a great crisis must come. This morning my father was driven abroad by Jeremiah and it appears that they were set upon by the mob with stones in the main street of the town. My father would say nothing of the encounter but the glass is broke in both the slides and the black has a great cut about his left eye.

This afternoon comes Lawyer Grylls to me in great secrecy and agitation, begging that I will prevail upon my father not to go again into town until the present high feeling is abated. God grant that such a time may come!

September 12th. Friday.

Today I dined with my father, the first time I have done so these four weeks past. Though nothing was said yet I perceive that he knows I have his secret. What obligation I still have as well as the dictates of reason and expediency persuade me to attempt some discussion touching that which lies between us that we may essay together some joint plan. But when I would speak there rises up before me the recollection of that terrible room and the vision of those innocent wretches who suffered there, so that I am overborne by my weakness and must keep silent. God forgive me and fit me for worse to come!

My father watches me closely yet not as one who fears or is cast down by a sense of guilt. He regards me with interest,

51

with seeming amusement, as one may look upon the engaging though unpredictable behaviour of a child.

September 16th. Tuesday.
It is four days since I last wrote in my diary and I do so now in the hope that I may obtain some ease of mind thereby. I have done what was needful to be done and I pray God make me ready to bear the consequences of it in this world and the next for I do not see how I could have done otherwise.

'Are you asleep, Henry?' He was lying back in his chair his eyes closed.
'Certainly not!'
'It looks as though Edward was right, doesn't it?'
Henry said nothing so she went on reading, her tiredness almost gone.

On the morning of Saturday I was visited again by Mr. Grylls who informed me that there was a move afoot amongst the rabble to storm the house and burn it to the ground. He entreated me to seek the protection of the Military but this I would by no means be persuaded to. Such action would the more excite the mob and would lead to closer inquiry into the reasons and justification for the unrest, the which I must at any cost avoid. He was greatly perturbed and said that his man, Rawley, had certain intelligence that the raid was planned to take place that very night. I settled his fears as best I could for I was already resolved upon the course I must take and when he was gone I set about my preparations.
My father supped at six, a habit acquired in his later years. He was accustomed to drink heavily at this meal then he would retire to his room for the night, rising at first light. Suffice it to say that I caused a quantity of opium to be added to his food and drink so that he might sleep the more readily and with greater depth. At first I feared that my plan had miscarried for after the meal he became animated

and talked with a freedom and in a manner that I had not known for many years but as the anodyne exerted its power he became drowsy, complained of an aching head and required to be helped up the stairs to his bed.

I had already posted a man on horseback along the road from the town so that I might have good notice of any threatening approach for I was resolved to take no irrevocable step until I was assured that the circumstances admitted of no other course.

During the afternoon it had come on to blow a great gale of wind and by nine o'clock I was convinced that the enterprise had been abandoned but scarcely had the last stroke died away when my messenger arrived with the news that upwards of thirty men had set out from the town bearing with them axes, bars and sledges as well as torches with a great quantity of tar and tallow. I knew that I must act.

My father was lying on his back, very pale, but breathing slow deep breaths which caused his frame to shudder at each exhalation. I took a pillow and applied it to his nostrils and mouth and held it there with all my strength. He did not struggle. I cannot say how long it was that I stayed there but when I removed the pillow I knew that he was dead. I straightened the bedclothes and went downstairs to give the news of his death to the servants.

At a quarter to ten a commotion at some distance from the house told me that the mob was near so with a lantern in my hand I went out on to the terrace to meet them. The wind had abated somewhat but it was still strong and their torches flared wildly as they made their way down the avenue towards the house. They drew up in an orderly manner at the foot of the steps and stood quietly while one of their number stepped forward with the intention of addressing me but I forestalled him. Shouting above the wind, I said: 'I know why you are here; there is no need for speeches. The fewer words spoken the better. My father is dead!'

They were hushed for a moment then one of them shouted, 'It's a trick!' Other voices joined him and there was a general movement forward but I held up my hand and they wavered. 'If you fear being tricked,' I shouted, 'you may see for yourselves. Appoint two or three of your number to accompany me and they shall see my father's body.'

There was a muttered consultation and two men were thrust forward, sheepish and unwilling, but they followed me to my father's room. At the door they would have stayed but I made them come into the room where the women were doing the last offices for my father's corpse. They stood for a moment, wild eyed, then turned on their heels and fled back to their fellows. I must confess to feeling sorrow for them for never had hatred a better cause or violence a greater justification.

In the morning one of my men found the body of Jeremiah, the black mute, hanging from a tree in the park.

The ways of God are not the ways of men but it is the hope of my soul that in all this I have been no more than the instrument of His Justice.

She finished reading. 'So Roger was a murderer too! Do you think that's what Lucy meant by the *inherited taint*?'

Henry stirred in his chair. 'You heard that? It could be I suppose but it hardly seems likely. After all, Roger was her great-great-grandfather. I should want more recent evidence of instability, even of homicidal traits, before I started worrying.'

'Perhaps she's got it—evidence, I mean.'

Henry nodded. 'Perhaps. This room—this terrible room— which upset Roger so much that he was prepared to murder his father, I wonder if it still exists.' He got up and moved over to the window, drew back the curtains and stood, looking out over the park. A pale moon riding high in a clear sky shining down on a white waste. 'I wonder if these are the only missing pages.'

Susan reminded him that in Roger's time the family still lived in the mansion, but he said nothing.

The seconds ticked by and she thought he would never turn round but at last he did. 'It was Joseph who built the Pavilion and the Willow Garden, wasn't it?' He didn't want an answer. 'Roger seems to have been a conscientious diarist so it's likely that he recorded his finding of the room, don't you think? I'm going to take a look.'

'I'll come with you.'

He stood over her grinning. 'I thought you were tired.'

'I am but I can manage to keep awake for another ten minutes.' In fact she had passed the nadir, her spirits were rising.

Easy to move about this house in silence. Good joinery and carpets everywhere. 'A housebreaker's paradise,' Henry whispered.

Portraits of bygone Vanes on the stairs, ghostly in the torchlight. A single Elizabethan ruff but a galaxy of Stuart gallantry, plumed hats, periwigs. No Leighs. You'd think they were renting the place.

At the door of the library Henry flicked switches and lights started up and out in the various bays until he came to the right one. The chest was still there at any rate. Henry opened it and removed the trays, then he reached down for the diaries. He lifted out three volumes. 'That's the lot! We're too late.'

'Somebody's playing games with us,' Susan said.

Henry put the trays back but kept the diaries and tucked them under his arm. 'If it's a game, I wish I knew the rules.'

Susan still couldn't believe that all this hocus pocus had anything to do with the missing girls.

At her door he stopped and kissed her quickly on the forehead. 'Good night! Merry Christmas!'

She slept and dreamed that Gerald North was chasing her round the Willow Garden brandishing a grid-iron. It seemed that she had scarcely closed her eyes when she was awakened by knocking. Broad daylight and Flossie with morning tea.

'A happy Christmas, Flossie.'

'The same to you, miss.' Wooden-faced, uncommunicative, she swished back the curtains.

Susan blinked in the sunshine. 'This house must keep you busy with only a daily girl to help.'

'Hard work never hurt anybody that I'd heard tell of,'

Flossie said. Strange to hear the old Victorian bromide trotted out. 'In any case, I could have plenty of help if I wanted it.' She glanced professionally round the room to see that all was as it should be.

Flossie seemed unlikely to encourage gossip but Susan decided to try her luck.

'I wouldn't say thank you for it!' Flossie said, her thoughts still on the subject of help. 'Young Sarah is more trouble than she's worth.'

'What happened to the first Mrs. Vane?' Shock tactics.

A cold stare. 'She died.'

'A long time ago?'

'A long time ago.' Brusque. But she didn't go away. She stood by the bed, watching Susan drink her tea.

'She died in a lunatic asylum, poor innocent young lady.'

'Innocent?'

'Well, it wasn't her fault was it?'

Susan tried again. 'You knew her, then?'

She made a gesture of impatience. 'Of course, I knew her! I've been with the family since I was fourteen.'

'With the Leighs.'

'Who else?'

'But I was talking about the first Mrs. Vane.'

'So was I. Sir Francis's sister, poor soul.'

'His sister! So he really is uncle to the Vane children, Beth and Johnny?'

She didn't bother with that one. It was difficult. 'I understood that Harold Vane came here when he returned from Malaya?'

Flossie nodded. 'So he did. But he only went there after his wife died, and the children stayed here.'

Not quite Lucy's story. At least not the impression she had left. No wonder she didn't want kids! 'And the second Mrs. Vane?'

An almost imperceptible jerk of the head and pursing of the lips. 'I've got work to do, miss!' And she was gone.

Susan washed and dressed and had breakfast alone, wondering what to do until Henry got up.

When she came out of the dining-room there was a stranger in the hall, a tall, elderly man with his back to her. Iron-grey hair and a navy blue overcoat, vaguely familiar, then he turned toward her. 'Susan!'

'Mr. Judd!' Detective Superintendent Judd, an old friend. 'Is Henry here?'

Susan told him and he looked put out. 'That's awkward, I'm here to see Sir Francis and it isn't about eighteenth-century books.'

'So you've found your own way here. I intended to get in touch with you this morning.' To Susan's surprise it was Henry coming from the direction of the kitchen—looking, astonishingly for the time of day, full of seasonable goodwill. 'A happy Christmas, John! Come with me, we can talk in the library.'

Judd's response lacked warmth. 'I'm here to see Sir Francis.'

'As you wish.'

'Be reasonable, Henry!' But Henry was already halfway to the library. Judd grinned. 'He doesn't change does he?'

'He doesn't improve at any rate,' Susan said.

Henry perched himself on the edge of one of the tables like a malevolent gargoyle on his favourite drainpipe. 'You are here about these missing girls?'

Judd nodded. 'In a way.'

'You know that somebody is trying to link their disappearance with a series of crimes alleged to have been committed by a Leigh ancestor?'

Judd fumbled with his moustache. 'I've heard plenty of wild rumours and now we've had a crackpot letter drawing our attention to some real or imagined Bluebeard character who lived at the time of the flood and suggesting that one of the present generation is setting up in the same line of business. The letter also states that similar communications had been sent to members of the family.'

'Well?'

'Well what? We haven't taken it seriously. You of all people must know that we are plagued by kinks.'

'But you've come here to know if Sir Francis wants you

to take action. Sir Francis is Chairman of the Bench and a member of the Police Authority so you have to go carefully.'

Judd was unruffled. 'That's not fair, Henry, and you know it. Sir Francis is the injured party in the matter of these letters and it's up to him to decide whether he wants anything done about it.'

'You could act on the letter you received.'

'We could, but it isn't usual.'

Henry's manner relaxed. 'Take off that damned overcoat and sit down, you look like something out of the cruel sea.'

The Superintendent took off his overcoat, folded it neatly and sat down. Henry peered down at him. 'It's obvious you don't think that there was anything sinister in the disappearances.'

'No, I don't. The only unusual feature was the fact that both girls left without telling their parents that they were going, but this seems to be amply accounted for by a long history of domestic troubles which made life at home for both the girls intolerable.'

'You've made no attempt to find them?'

'No. The girls are of age to go where they like. Nobody has reported them as missing persons and the parents are only too anxious to avoid talk.'

'But you did try the bus and railway stations and you did ask local beat coppers to keep their ears and eyes open?'

Judd's eyes twinkled. 'Routine with no result. And that means nothing!'

Henry nodded. 'But it does mean something that our unknown letter-writer is trying to make people believe there was dirty work.'

'That,' said Judd, 'is another story.'

'You know Sir Francis's reputation?'

'In what respect?'

'Girls.'

Judd looked distressed. 'Really, Henry! In the man's own house! He's not under investigation.'

'But you do know?'

'I know nothing; like everybody else I've heard gossip.'

'Which says what?'

The Superintendent looked uneasily toward the door. 'That they can't keep a servant sleeping-in, except the old house-keeper.'

'And?'

'There was a scandal a year or two back involving a school-girl. The story goes that it cost him a big sum of money to keep it out of our hands.'

'Ah! There you are!' Sir Francis breezed in, beaming and like a baby fresh from his bath—shining. 'I'm so glad you've got together. The Superintendent is an old friend and I know that you two have been—shall I say colleagues?—in the past.' Smooth as silk, but a lingering impression that he wasn't as pleased as he made out.

'I'm sorry to disturb you on Christmas morning, sir, but if I could have a word with you in private?'

Raised eyebrows. 'Surely, Superintendent . . . !'

Judd smiled. 'Well, it's up to you, sir, of course. We have received an anonymous letter making certain accusations concerning the missing girls.'

Leigh sobered. 'I expected that. As Dr. Pym will tell you, there have been similar letters addressed to me and to other members of this household.'

'Over what period, sir?'

Sir Francis frowned. 'About a month.'

'The proper course would have been to pass the letters on to the police, sir.'

Sir Francis was stiff. 'You must allow me to be the judge of that, Superintendent. It is up to you to decide whether or not the accusations are worth investigating but the letters are my affair.'

Judd opened his mouth to speak but Henry forestalled him. 'You are quite right, Sir Francis, but while Mr. Judd is here I want to tell him and you of a curious incident which concerns my car.' He related the story of the bent bumper and the extra mileage, then he produced three little plastic envelopes from his wallet. He emptied the contents of the first one on to a sheet of paper: a few crumbs of peaty soil and several small sharp-edged chips of rock. From the second envelope he shook out three plant fragments, a bit of heather, a tiny sprig of gorse and a few blades of dried grass. Sir Francis watched him mystified, Judd polished his spectacles in the manner of a politician registering non-involvement. Henry looked around at his audience. 'I recovered these from the tire treads of my car and from the damaged bumper and number plate. Black peaty soil; chips of quartz stained with iron salts; fragments of a rock known locally as blue elvan and bits of three different plant species.' He picked up each of the plants in turn. 'Heather or ling (*Calluna vulgaris*); gorse (*Ulex europaeus*); and blades of the grass *Festuca ovina*, bleached as it often is at this time of the year on cliff tops. All from a locality within a dozen miles of here.' He looked at Sir Francis. 'I expect you could place it for us?'

Beaming smile. 'How interesting! I think I can!' He got up, crossed to a desk in another bay and returned with an ordnance map and a scale. He spread the map on the table and placed the scale with its zero on the town. 'There you are, eleven and a quarter miles as a crow flies, the cliffs on the north side of St. Piran's Bay. Derelict mine workings, plenty of old shafts and a network of mine roads, rough but still passable in a car.'

Henry waited, looking smug. The Superintendent stopped polishing his glasses, put them on and studied the fragments with a disparaging air. 'Interesting. What are they supposed to mean? Perhaps one of the garage lads borrowed your car and took his girl friend out on to the cliffs. It's happened before.'

Henry opened his third envelope and let the gold cross slip on to the pile of debris. The effect on Judd was gratifying if you were in Henry's corner.

'Where did you get that?'

Henry told him.

'The Ford girl had a cross like that. Her mother mentioned it.'

Henry turned the cross over, 'It's inscribed, G.F. 1962.'

Judd nodded. 'That's it, Gillian Ford, but she disappeared

more than a month ago!'

In the silence Susan could hear a radio somewhere in the house—carols.

Judd was the first to speak. 'It can't be coincidence that your car was used but it must have been taken from Marsden's garage.'

'They leave the cars parked outside when they're not actually working on them . . .' Sir Francis volunteered.

'With the ignition keys in?' Judd snapped.

Sir Francis flushed at Judd's tone. 'Not to my knowledge.'

The Superintendent stared at the cross as though it mesmerized him. 'That puts a different complexion on the whole affair, we shall have to find out how it came to be in your car, Henry.'

Leigh eyed the cross with almost ludicrous astonishment. 'Does this mean that these girls really have been . . . I just can't grasp it.'

Judd stood up. 'We shall have to organize a search, we can't ignore the possibility.' He turned to Henry. 'Perhaps you would avoid using your car for the present, I want our chaps to go over it . . .'

Henry nodded. '. . . with a fine-tooth comb, I know.'

When they were alone, Henry said, 'Now, Susan, we will take our own look at these shafts before his policemen start tramping all over the place.'

'Mr. Judd wants his men to go over the car.'

'Then we'll ask Sir Francis to lend us his.'

CHAPTER SIX

THREE MILES OUTSIDE the town the roads were clear of snow and sunshine conspired with the car heater in deception. For the first time since leaving *Peel* Susan could relax and think about something other than keeping the car out of the ditch. Was it feasible that this girl, missing for a month, had been in their car two nights ago? And if so, was she dead or alive? There seemed to be only one answer to that. Sir Francis had mentioned derelict mine workings and old shafts —it seemed obvious what Henry was expecting to find. But where had she been for a month? Who drove the car? And why Henry's? Above all, what had it got to do with the Leighs?

Henry broke in on her thoughts, 'How far have you got? Have you asked yourself why, if she was in the car, was she kept alive for a month—and where?'

'We don't know that she was kept alive. As far as I can see, she might have been killed at any time since she disappeared.'

Henry shrugged. 'If she travelled in our car she hasn't been long dead.'

'I don't see . . .'

'My dear Susan! You a zoologist! Do you think that a corpse more than a few days old . . . ?'

He was right, of course.

Somehow it made it worse to think that this girl might have died in the very recent past. She told him about her conversation with Flossie but he offered no comment and for the rest of their journey he was silent and thoughtful.

They were entering St. Piran, a single street snaking round the base of the carn. The church bells tumbled down the scale in cheerful, monotonous repetition but the street was deserted. Glimpses of decorated trees and flickering firelight through the parted curtains of the windows seemed incongruous in the sunshine. Beyond the village they turned off, up a side road, toward the sea. A newly made up road between two lines of box-like bungalows, then open country and mine dumps, their rawness scarcely concealed by the sparse vegetation.

If Gillian Ford was dead, what about Eileen Cassels? Incredible on this bright Christmas morning, to think that a girl could be held against her will at the mercy of a psychopath. And yet children have been kidnapped, tortured and murdered in a suburban house with nobody apparently, the wiser. Susan remembered a schoolgirl phase when every

62

moment of happiness or even contentment was marred by guilt arising from an awareness of human suffering—'At this moment, while I sit here . . .'—Of course it didn't last long, the mind makes its own self-preserving adjustments and our sympathies are focused on a contracted field. But for a moment, she was sickened by the thought that while Henry indulged his petulance and the superintendent studied protocol, this girl might die. It wasn't fair, of course; the special position of a surgeon, a teacher or a policeman, doesn't turn a human being into a saint nor does emotional involvement make for clear thinking.

The road turned at right angles and they were running parallel with the sea, separated from it by a quarter of a mile of more or less level moorland pockmarked by shafts, some walled, others, like craters guarded only by low mounds of bramble covered mine-waste. Nearer the cliffs three or four ruined engine houses, their stacks truncated, stabbed like jagged teeth into the great band of featureless blue sea. Susan turned the car on to a broad stony track which seemed to bisect the wilderness and after a hundred yards she pulled in on to short springy turf and shut off the engine.

'What now?'

Henry seemed to come back from far away. 'You said last night that somebody was playing games with us and I think you may be right. I can't get away from the feeling that we are being fed with information.'

'Like the clues in Lucy's treasure hunt.'

He laughed. 'They led somewhere.' He seemed to take in their surroundings for the first time. 'This is as good a place as any, we can walk from here.'

Out of the car it was bitterly cold, a northerly wind blowing off the sea armed with icicles. Susan had a lined oilskin coat but Henry grumbled that his overcoat was no more use than a net curtain. He studied the landscape, morose, gloomy. 'There must be a score or more of shafts and we can't expect them to climb down them all so we shall have to narrow the search. The car must have been driven here on Tuesday night when it was raining so there is a chance of tire marks.'

They walked down the track until they came to another, crossing the first, then they split up. 'Keep to paths you could take a car down and pay special attention to those which pass near shafts.'

The place was a network of tracks though most of them were too narrow for a car; even so it was going to take a long time to cover the ground. Half an hour later they were still exploring offshoots of the original track, some of which ended in cleared areas used by picknickers while others skirted a couple of shafts only to peter out in the heather or branch into a complex of footways. At any rate the vegetation was right—heather and gorse, dwarfed by salt winds and poor soil, and sheep's fescue, much of it bleached and mummified. The exercise was warming, and provided they were not walking directly into the wind it wasn't too unpleasant. Despite the impression of level moorland there were plenty of hollows and in them, cut off from the wind, it was almost spring-like. Coming up out of one of the hollows, Susan saw Henry signalling to her, a couple of hundred yards to seaward.

She joined him by a walled shaft, the wall, as usual, built on a mound of spewed out rubble overgrown by gorse and difficult to reach. The shaft was a little distance from any track with an intervening expanse of half frozen black mud. Henry pointed to two good tire impressions on the margin of the mud and Susan thought they looked familiar which meant almost nothing. Henry picked up a stone and lobbed it over the wall of the shaft. A dull thud as though it had fallen on to a carpet of vegetation. He tried another with the same result.

'It looks as though they covered this one in.'

Many of the mineral exploiters had been content to rip the guts out of the land and leave it an eyesore and a menace but some with an elementary regard for public safety walled and covered their disused shafts.

'Do you think her body is here?'

Henry said nothing.

'Room for one more?' Edward Leigh. They hadn't heard him coming along the path against the wind.

Henry was curt. 'Your brother told you we were here, Mr. Leigh?'

'You could say that; I had to twist his arm a bit, Francis can be bloody tiresome over trifles.' His manner was as flippant as usual but he was wary, trying to sum up what was going on. 'Do you think the girl is in that shaft?'

'No.'

'Because there are no footprints to go with the tire marks?'

'You are very observant.'

Edward eyed the shaft. 'That one is covered—I know, I used to spend a lot of time here a few years back.'

'Doing what?' Susan felt the need to fill in the gaps left by Henry's silences.

'Sketching. I worked up quite a few pictures from this . . .' He gestured vaguely. 'Rape of a fair country angle. I even sold some.' He searched in the pockets of his tattered anorak and came out with a crushed packet of cigarettes. 'Here! Do yourself an injury.'

Henry's look was withering but it had no effect on Edward. He turned his back to the wind, lit a cigarette, then took up the conversation where it had been left off—more or less. 'But whoever it was must have had some reason for driving your car all the way out here on a filthy winter's night.'

'I suppose so.'

Edward winked at Susan, then crossed the mud to the shaft, picking his way gingerly. After prospecting for a moment he hoisted himself through the clinging gorse on to the wall. Two or three big stones dislodged from the top slid down to the mud.

'Idiot!' Henry said. 'Serves him right if he breaks his neck!'

Edward disappeared over the wall but he was gone only a moment, then he reappeared, carrying a bundle, something rolled up in plastic and tied with string. He slid back to the ground, crossed the mud and offered the bundle to Henry. 'Is this what you wanted?'

'What's in it?' Henry took the parcel holding it gingerly by the string.

'How the hell should I know?'

'You seemed to know where to find it, so it was hardly unreasonable to suppose that you might know what was in it.'

Edward's blue eyes widened. 'You're deliberately trying to needle me. But you're wasting your time, I've got a hide like a politician's.'

Henry was suave as ever. 'You mistake me, Mr. Leigh.'

'Like hell, I do! But never mind that, what you don't seem to realize is that I'm on your side, I want to help.'

Henry smiled. 'I'm glad to hear it. In that case, you won't object to telling me where you were the night before last.'

Edward's manner changed. 'The night before last? The night someone pinched your car and drove out here to dump this lot—is that it?'

'And just possibly Gillian Ford's body as well.'

Edward gave him an appraising look. 'But you don't think so, do you?'

'Did you know the girl?'

'In the way of business; she sat for me a few times, though she didn't want her father to find out.'

'And on the night?'

'I was visiting a friend.'

'By car?'

'Yes.'

'Your own or your brother's?'

'Mine—the Mini.'

'Could you prove that if you had to?'

Edward was shaken. 'I doubt it. I arrived back at the cottage around eleven and slept in a virtuous bed which doesn't help, does it?'

Henry stood, staring at the ground, his hands thrust deep into the pockets of his overcoat. It was bitterly cold, no shelter from the wind off the sea. Edward stamped his feet and Susan shrank into her oilskin, frozen and tense.

Henry glanced at the bundle. 'Well, it looks as though we've got what we came for.'

Edward had parked his car behind Sir Francis's. He climbed in, reversed off the grass on to the track with a sputtering screech of ti res. 'If you follow me I'll take you a shorter way.

66

I'll go slow so that you don't rattle Frankie's old crate too much.'

'Insufferable young ape!' Henry muttered.

As they emerged from the heathland on to the road Susan spotted a police car and a red painted Land Rover parked away to their left. She drew Henry's attention.

'I saw them.'

'I expect they're looking for us.' She drove to the parked cars which were deserted except for a constable on radio watch.

Henry gave him the bundle. 'For Superintendent Judd with Dr. Pym's compliments.'

Susan had her work cut out manoeuvring the big car through narrow lanes after the scuttling Mini but in a surprisingly short space of time they were passing once more under the arrogant Vane bears. Not far inside the main gates Edward turned off toward his cottage and they arrived at the house alone.

'Leave the car, in case we need it,' Henry said.

Lucy met them in the hall, she was composed, giving no sign of anything untoward. Henry made some banal remark about the weather and she told them that lunch would be ready in half an hour. They might have been house guests returning from a brisk walk before lunch.

Lunch was depressing. Sir Francis was not there and Lucy explained that he was confined to his room by a minor indisposition.

Gerald's thin lips twisted into a smile. 'Francis is suffering from Urticaria—nettle rash. I understand that the rash is usually occasioned by an allergic response to certain protein foods but in this case it appears to be nervous in origin. The symptoms appear whenever he is subject to emotional stress.' A dry chuckle. 'Embarrassing for him—and very inconvenient!'

Lucy was not amused. 'Poor daddy! He has been subject to these attacks for some time and it is difficult to find the cause. Fortunately one of the antihistamine drugs brings fairly rapid relief and he should be presentable again in a few hours.'

'We have another family party this evening,' Gerald remarked to his plate, 'and Francis would hate to miss that.'

Flossie came in with a trolley to remove their soup plates and serve the meat course. In the silence which followed Gerald crumbled a bread roll with his fingers absentmindedly. 'Are you a believer in psychosomatic phenomena, Dr. Pym?'

Henry was brusque. 'I hardly know what it means. Surely there is a continuing interaction between our mental and our physical processes, the two are inseparable. At what point such interaction can be said to give rise to psychosomatic phenomena I have never understood. I know that I am likely to suffer from indigestion and possibly ulcers if I am subjected to continuing mental stress, I know that I shall blush if I am embarrassed but . . .'

Gerald interrupted with the smooth polish of an advocate. 'I had in mind more dramatic manifestations—faith healing, healing by hypnotic suggestion.'

Henry was making a dexterous dissection of the leg muscles of a chicken and answered without interrupting this activity. 'I know very little of either but since the work of Charcot at Satpêtrière the value of hypnosis in the treatment of certain psychological conditions seems to have been established. It is not uncommon for such conditions to be accompanied by organic symptoms.'

Gerald North laughed. 'It seems to me that scientists are even more wary than lawyers. But you should talk to Harold Vane on the subject. He would make far more sweeping claims.'

Susan had the strong impression that Gerald had just come to the point, his reason for introducing the topic in the first place. Henry was silent and to bridge the gap she asked, 'Is he knowledgeable about hypnosis?'

Gerald nodded. 'Yes, I think you could say so. Surprising, isn't it? He doesn't seem the type. While he was in Kuala Lumpur he came under the influence of a certain Indian gentleman, a Dr. Bannerjea, who, on Harold's evidence, must be either a very great man or a very great rogue. At any rate, he introduced Harold to a curious group of people full of esoteric lore and the impression they made on him has been lasting.'

'Does Mr. Vane practise hypnosis?' Henry demanded.

North laughed. 'When he gets the chance. Helen is one of his victims and, fortunately for him, she is an excellent deep trance subject. So is Francis but Francis does not approve and, as far as I know, has only once allowed himself to be a guinea pig.' He sipped water from his glass then patted his lips with a napkin. 'One interesting point on which Harold differs from the accepted authorities is in his assertion that a hypnotized subject may be caused to perform acts which are harmful to him or which he would regard as immoral or improper if he were in full control of his mental processes.'

Henry placed his knife and fork side by side on his empty plate and sat back in his chair. 'That is very interesting. Ericksen's work seems to demonstrate the contrary but I have often thought that more experimental evidence is needed.'

North looked at him with apparent interest. 'You must certainly talk to Harold. I think I am right in saying that English law recognizes the possibility of rape during hypnotic sleep.'

'Now, for goodness sake, let's change the subject!' Lucy said.

When lunch was over and they were going upstairs, Susan said, 'What was all that about?'

'I've no idea.'

'He seemed anxious to make his point.'

'Yes, he did.'

And that was all.

'Shall we be working in the library this afternoon?'

Henry seemed preoccupied. 'What? No. I'm pretty sure that Judd will come here after he has cavorted round the mine dumps for an hour or two and I want to talk to him. Perhaps you would like to amuse yourself.' He added as an afterthought: 'Susan—if you go out about the estate, do get back before it is dark.'

'I'm a big girl.'

'I've noticed. It worries me.'

Susan went to her room wondering how she would spend the afternoon of Christmas Day. She thought of reading in front of the fire but the silence of the house oppressed her. She had a yearning for companionship and decided to go for a walk. She put on her fur lined boots, duffle coat and hood and set out. The sun was hidden by a ceiling of high cloud, the wind seemed even colder and the snow was crisp under foot. She crossed the park to the *Pinetum*, made her way through the wood with little difficulty and came out on to the rhododendron slope and the Willow Garden. A landscape with the muted colours of a Hokusai print. Snow lay thick on the roof tiles of the Pavilion and the Mandarin's house, it etched the sweeping limbs of the great willow and the carved rail of the little bridge beneath.

This was the place of her first encounter with Edward and she half expected, half hoped to be greeted now with some cheerful inanity but there was no one. He had given her an open invitation to the cottage and she was tempted, but reluctant to start an affair which might make difficulties if she stayed at *Peel* for any length of time. All the same she discovered that she had decided to walk in the general direction of the cottage. She had set foot on the bridge when something caused her to look back at the Mandarin's house. There was Johnny, standing in the angle of the porch wall, statuesque, monumental; like a Ming warrior, guardian of the gate. Susan lifted her hand in greeting but though he was looking directly at her he gave no sign of recognition or acknowledgment. It was unnerving to be watched as a naturalist watches his quarry —without communication. She crossed the bridge and walked to the top of the opposite slope before looking back. He was gone and though there was very little cover she had the uncomfortable feeling that he was close at hand. It took all her resolution to enter the belt of trees which separated her from the estate road to the cottage. But she did not see him again and in five minutes she was in sight of the cottage. Edward was standing at the gate.

'Waiting for someone?'

'You.'

'You must have been there a long time.'

'Actually I was looking for Johnny, he usually turns up just after lunch but he hasn't been today.'

Susan told him that she had seen the boy at the Mandarin's house and he looked mildly concerned. 'There's something upsetting Johnny and I've no idea what it is. I'm a bit worried about him. However, come in, I knew you wouldn't be able to hold out for long.'

Edward's living-room occupied the whole frontage of his house. Red tiled floor with Persian rugs, their colours glowing. White walls with Utamaro prints, heavy oak furniture with the patina of age. Little evidence of privation and none of his pictures. Susan was surprised and pleased. 'You like it?'

'What Wordsworth called, "A refined rusticity". Yes, I like it very much.'

He took her coat, fussing over her. Now that she was his guest he seemed to become nervous, almost shy. 'Something to drink?'

She laughed. 'I've just had lunch.'

'Of course. Let's just sit and talk then.'

'Do you look after yourself? Get your own meals and do your own housework?' Susan was intrigued by the spotless neatness of everything.

'I share a daily with the Vanes—a morbidly efficient woman —she is responsible for this unnatural disinfected deodorized and polished exhibition cage. If you are interested in the real me, I live upstairs.'

They went upstairs to his workroom. 'Don't call it a studio, only photographers and male whores have studios any more.' The room was under the roof with a sloping ceiling a good chunk of which had been removed to give a north light, but there was a long low window facing south as well, looking out over the trees. A bare room, as big as the one below. Two easels, several plank bookcases stuffed with books, a stack of prepared hardboard sheets, a few canvases on stretchers, a couch and a bed. The floor was uncarpeted and flecked with paint of every imaginable colour. A slow combustion stove glowed cosily through its red mica windows.

He put her to sit on the couch but sat on the floor himself, his hands clasped round his knees. He wore the black trousers and pullover he had worn to the party and he looked oddly juvenile. Susan felt protective toward him but at the same time slightly repelled.

'You don't splash your pictures around.'

He drew a crushed packet of cigarettes from his trouser pocket and lit one. 'I can't bear to look at the bloody things except in short sharp doses. I can't understand people who put their own pictures on the walls, it's like wallowing in your own vomit.'

'You have a charming imagery all your own.'

He chuckled. 'You must think we're a bloody queer lot.'

'You do your best to create that impression.'

He sprang lightly to his feet, like an athlete. 'Judge for yourself.' He whisked a hardboard sheet from a stack by the wall and propped it on the easel. For a moment Susan had the impression of an intriguing blend of blues with no discernible form; then, as she continued to study the board, a female form seemed to grow out of the colour, to emerge and finally to dominate it. The figure was conventional though the pose was not. Before she had had a chance to analyse her impressions he had replaced the picture with another. This time it was a study in flaming reds, and again, after an interval, the features of a female figure seemed to crystallize out of swirling vortices of colour. The contours of the body were defined by tonal changes which were also a part of the broader geometric pattern of the whole. What struck Susan most was that the convolutions of this pattern were more sensuous, more suggestive than the nude figure itself.

'That is one of the missing girls—Eileen Cassels—the first to disappear.'

It was not a likeness for police identification purposes but Susan had little doubt that she would know the girl if she saw her in the context of the case. 'Why the reds? Any significance?'

Edward smiled. 'I use colours which I believe to be appropriate to the sitter. This girl was a sexual bomb, she only needed a match applied to the blue touch paper or perhaps I should be less archaic if I said she simply needs the right fuse.'

'And nobody had run the risk to date?'

'I'm sure they hadn't.' He removed the picture and reached for the next. 'Well?'

'Well, what?'

'If you are a woman at all your next question will be "What colour do you see me"?'

Susan laughed. 'You have an insufferable conceit of yourself.'

He put his next painting up. 'This is different.'

It was. A straight painting, a nude girl facing the painter in a relaxed professional stance, hands on hips. But there were two bizarre features: from her parted lips a trail of flowers emerged to disappear in diminishing perspective over her shoulder and several gay peacock butterflies (*Nymphalis io*) fluttered round the triangle of her pubic hair. It was Helen Vane. Susan was startled by the cruelty of the painting.

'You are not Botticelli,' she said.

'You don't like it?'

'I think it is vicious.'

Edward grinned. 'It was intended to be but dear Helen liked it. She is so stupid she hardly seems real.'

'I doubt if her husband would appreciate it.'

'No, I doubt if he would. Whatever else Harold may be he is not stupid.'

He showed her perhaps a dozen more of his pictures, most were like the first two in subject and treatment, the rest were more traditional and included one of Beth Vane. Little more than a coloured sketch but it had an exquisite delicacy appropriate to the youth and manifest innocence of the girl. She sat on a kitchen chair, naked to the waist, an art school pose.

'You live dangerously,' Susan said.

He put the painting away, frowning. 'Fortunately I am a painter first and a lecher second.'

'I'd better be getting back.'

He looked at his watch. 'Stay and have some tea with me, then we can go across to this damned party together. You can ring your boss if you want to and ask him to let you off the lead for a bit longer.'

She telephoned the house and spoke to Flossie. 'Dr. Pym is in the library with the police superintendent, miss. Shall I put you through?'

'No, I simply wanted to say that I shall not be in to tea but I shall be coming along with Mr. Edward to the party.'

They got the tea together in a poky little kitchen behind the sitting-room then they took it upstairs on trays. 'I like this room,' Susan said.

Edward nodded as he licked chocolate from his fingers. 'Most things which grow are better than things which are made.'

'You are worried about these missing girls—I mean personally worried, you and your brother.'

Edward shrugged. 'Yes, I suppose so. Francis doesn't confide in me but I certainly am, it's not very pleasant to be accused of abducting and murdering girls.'

'I wouldn't have thought either of you were the sort to be unduly bothered by a couple of anonymous letters and some malicious gossip.'

Edward emptied his cup and refilled it. 'There's more to it than that. Somebody went to the trouble of digging up that yarn about Joseph and linking it with the disappearances. That story isn't well known outside the family and you saw what happened last night. Whoever is responsible for the disappearances there is someone in the family making capital out of it.'

He sat staring out of the window. The darkening sky above the trees had a faint rosy flush and the light in the room was fading. The clock downstairs chimed and struck five. Suddenly he turned to face her, 'Do you ever feel doubts of your own sanity?'

He was serious and she answered him seriously. 'I suppose everybody has moments of doubt.'

'But nagging continuing uncertainty?'

'No.'

He shook his head. 'Of course you don't. But you would

74

if you belonged to a family like ours. Never mind about ancestry, just look at us as we are. Look at Johnny—his mother—my sister. She died in a lunatic asylum after crouching for months in the corner of a room never moving unless they moved her—they said that she presented a classic example of the withdrawal syndrome. Look at Lucy . . . !' He gestured as though words failed him. 'Although Lucy is my niece there is very little difference in our ages and we were brought up together like brother and sister. She was brilliant, a prodigy. She took Oxford by storm. A first, postgraduate work, a junior Fellowship—the lot! Then with no warning and for no reason that anybody knows she packs it in and comes home—to marry Gerald. Gerald!' He laughed. 'Of course, you know that Gerald is one of us?'

Susan shook her head.

'My cousin—eldest son of father's sister . . . And now, of course, Lucy is scared stiff of having kids.' He sat for a moment, staring at the multicoloured floorboards. 'Lucy was attractive, vivacious as well as intelligent, but look at her now—a little grey mouse who does her own housework and dabbles with the *Young Sisterhood* or some such obscene futility!'

Susan was at a loss. It is acutely embarrassing when the clown suddenly becomes serious, you cannot really believe in it and you wait for the pay-off.

Edward looked at her and grinned. 'I don't know why I tell you all this unless it's because I want you to know which strings make the puppet kick.'

A thought occurred to her. 'Edward, what *were* you doing in the garage on Christmas Eve night when I found Gillian Ford's cross?'

He grinned. 'I was looking for something—a handbag.'

'Did you find it?'

'No.' He shrugged. 'You might as well know the grizzly details. The evening before I'd committed the ultimate crime —pinching Gerald's car. Mine was in dock, one of the estate people had Francis's and I'd promised to take a friend out. There wasn't much risk, for Gerald rarely uses his car at night

75

—anyway, I took a chance and all went well. But next morning she rang up to say she'd left her bloody handbag in the back. By that time, of course, Gerald had the car at his office so I took the first chance to look for the damn thing when he came home.'

'But you didn't find it?'

'No, the silly little cow must have dropped it somewhere else.'

'I see.'

Perhaps she sounded prim but in fact she was growing to like him, his strange mixture of exuberant vitality, cynicism and pathos. Not a recipe for a husband perhaps but an exhilarating companion. When they stood up she let him take her in his arms and kiss her on the lips.

'Remember that you are a painter first.'

'Green,' he whispered. 'Green, definitely.'

'Why green?'

But she got no answer.

They set out for the house at a little before seven, walking through the darkness. Edward would have taken his car but Susan dissuaded him. 'Let's walk. It doesn't take long through the Willow Garden, does it?'

'I suppose not but it won't be easy in the dark.' In fact, despite the pitch blackness of the sky, the snow made it easy to find their way.

As they were approaching the bridge and they could see before them a vague spectral outline of the great willow, Edward said, 'Nervous?'

'Not really. I should be if I were alone.'

He squeezed her arm. 'I don't think you have any need to worry.'

'Why not?'

'He doesn't go for blondes. Both girls had—have dark hair— jet black as far as my recollection goes.'

'You think that means something?'

'God knows!'

'Little Mei Mei is dark enough.'

'I know. I've drawn her attention to the fact—and Harold's.

It worries me.' They walked over the bridge. 'Look! A light in the Mandarin's house! There! No, it's gone . . .'

'I can't see anything.'

'It comes and goes, I think it's somebody with a torch.'

'Could it be Johnny?'

'It could, but I've never known him go inside the place alone. He always seems scared of the Garden.'

They were speaking in whispers and they had walked on until they reached the ornamental railing surrounding the house.

'Wait there, I'm going in to take a look.'

'Be careful.'

'Don't worry. I'm not likely to be mistaken for a luscious brunette. And I've got this.' He held out the four-cell torch he had brought but had not needed. 'Ten to one it's some tramp.'

Susan was left standing under the willow near the fringe of its great canopy. She moved toward the trunk so that she would be less conspicuous against the snow. The silence was almost complete. Once or twice a dog barked a long way off then she caught the sound of a band, it came and went in a tantalizing fashion carried by light movements of the air. But she identified the tune: *While shepherds watch'd their flocks by night.* She had forgotten that it was Christmas. Then the droning of an aeroplane. Edward seemed to have been gone a long time but she could hear nothing from the Mandarin's house. The cold crept up through her legs. She wondered if she ought to find her courage and go after him but the decision was taken from her hands. A thud, a crash and the tinkle of broken glass from the other side of the house, then Edward's voice bellowing, 'Come back you bastard!' She made her way round the outside of the house, sometimes ploughing through the soft soil of flower beds, at other times feeling hard gravel under the snow. Then she saw Edward standing in the snow about a hundred yards from the house, probing the darkness ahead with his torch. She called and he came reluctantly back. 'I lost him.'

'You're not hurt?'

'What? No, I didn't get within yards of him. There are plenty of places to hide in there with all the museum junk and I thought I'd do the rooms thoroughly one at a time. I'd done the outside room and started on the second when there was a god-almighty crash—you must have heard it. He'd busted open the double doors in the third room with a stool. They're never opened normally and I don't even know if there's a key . . . Anyway he got away.'

They went to inspect the damage. The most un-Chinese double doors were intact except for the glass panels which were splintered. They closed the doors without difficulty and wedged them. 'There! That'll have to do, there's nothing in there worth pinching anyway.'

CHAPTER SEVEN

PYM WENT TO the library after lunch to look for a folder of estate maps which he remembered seeing in one of the bays. He found it and opened it on one of the tables. The mustiness of age rose and engulfed him like a cloud. Maps and plans of the estate between 1690 and 1800 collected, according to the titular inscription, *by Joseph Leigh For the Instruction and Edification of his Heirs and Annotated in his Hand*. They were probably valuable as historical documents but Henry's interest in them was not antiquarian. When Judd arrived he was studying an estate plan of 1709.

'Look, the old mansion is shown here but the Dower House had not yet been built.' His finger ran over the map. 'The site must be about here where they show a ruined chapel. According to the stone over the door the Dower House dates from 1712.'

Judd put on his steel rimmed spectacles and stared at the map. 'Very interesting but I have other things on my mind.'

'The estate was a good deal smaller when they made this map—at least the enclosed park was smaller. The boundary
78

runs not far from this house; the *Pinetum* and the *Willow Garden* must have been enclosed later.'

Judd said nothing.

'The lake is new too; evidently they made it by damming back this little stream. There were mine workings—you see...' He took out a hand lens from his pocket to read the faded lettering *Tinn Works.*

Judd sat down and put his spectacles back in their case to emphasize his lack of interest. He drew out his pouch and pipe. 'Apart from your contribution we drew blank this morning.'

'What was in the bundle? Gillian Ford's clothes?'

Judd put a match to his tobacco. 'Just underclothes and the girls' parents can't identify them with any certainty.'

'That *is* odd!' Henry lost interest in the map and gave his undivided attention to the superintendent.

'The forensic chaps have been over your car and though I've not had their report yet, they're fairly sure that the cross is the only evidence we are likely to get.'

Henry studied the tips of his fingers as he often did when he was trying to work out a logical sequence in his mind. 'This bothers me. The finding of the cross made it a tenable hypothesis that Gillian Ford's body had been disposed of on the mine dumps but all we find is a bundle of unidentifiable clothing.'

Judd was unimpressed. 'You are making too much of it. If the girls have been murdered their killer has to dispose of them and their belongings . . .'

'But why bother with the clothes separately—and only underclothes? Surely his big problem is to get rid of the body or bodies, clothed or unclothed? Why use my car? And above all, why leave a trail that a half-wit could hardly miss? Is it likely that a readily identifiable object like that cross would be left behind by accident? It doesn't make sense.'

Judd smoked, unmoved by the battery of questions. 'I admit that it seems to stretch coincidence a bit far, but the alternative . . .'

'The alternative is that somebody is doing all this with his tongue in his cheek. To borrow a phrase from Susan's vocabulary, we are being taken for a ride.' Judd opened his mouth to speak but Henry cut him short. 'I have already come to that conclusion on other grounds. The problem is to distinguish between red herrings and fresh fish.'

'It could be that someone is trying to deflect attention away from *Peel*.'

'Away from *Peel*! Of one thing I'm certain, all this *hocus pocus* is to draw attention *to Peel* and its inmates, not away from it.'

'To back up the anonymous letters?'

Henry nodded. 'I suppose so.' He paused. 'Eileen Cassels—she was the first—tell me about her.'

Judd took a file from his briefcase and placed it on the table. With irritating deliberation he thumbed through the pages. 'Here we are: she was five foot four, a hundred and fifteen pounds, dark, pretty and twenty-one years old.'

'What was her job?'

'She was a nurse.'

'A nurse?'

Judd nodded. 'That's what I said.'

'What were the circumstances of her disappearance?'

Judd turned several pages which was all the more exasperating in that he had the facts at his fingertips. 'She came off duty at eight in the evening and she was expected to come straight home—fifteen minutes walk across the town.'

'So she would have been wearing her uniform?'

Judd sighed. 'No, the hospital rules require nurses to change when they come off duty. In any case she had taken a packed suitcase with her to the hospital that day; she was due for a few days leave and she told one of the other girls that she was spending it with friends. She didn't say where.'

'What are the parents like?'

Judd hesitated, staring at the bowl of his pipe. 'Come-to-Jesus—at least that's what we used to call them when I was a boy. They act on the assumption that whatever comes naturally must be wrong. She had a hell of a life of it, poor kid.'

'But she was of age and earning her own living, she could have walked out.'

A slow smile. Judd had a daughter of his own. 'There are still such things as filial respect and affection, Henry. But leaving that aside, she evidently intended to walk out.'

'How did her parents take it?'

'Prepared to believe the worst, and the worst in their view is that she's gone off with some man.'

Henry sitting, elbows on the arms of his chair, fingers matched as though in formal prayer, looked at Judd, 'Now tell me about Gillian Ford and for God's sake stop fiddling with those papers. I know it's an act.'

Judd smiled but he did not refer to his papers again. 'Gillian was five three, one hundred and twelve pounds, dark, pretty and twenty-one years old. She was a receptionist at one of the dentists.' Her parents have been separated more than once and the trouble seems to be that her mother drinks. Gillian has threatened to leave home more than once . . .'

'What were the circumstances of her disappearance?'

Judd relit his pipe before replying. 'It was toward the end of November, almost exactly a month after the other girl. Her parents were away for a few days celebrating their latest reconciliation and when they came back the girl was gone. She'd taken a suitcase and some clothes with her.'

'What exactly did she take?'

The superintendent's attention sharpened. 'I haven't got a list but I can see that it might be worth finding out—now that we have reason to suspect foul play.'

Henry got up and walked to the nearest window. He stood looking out, the scene like a line and wash drawing in blue-black ink, white and slate grey-blues. Judd continued to talk but it was impossible to judge whether Henry was paying attention.

'From their descriptions those girls might have been twins and both could walk out of their homes without causing much surprise. Both sets of parents are more concerned to avoid scandal than to find them—a fine recipe for a kidnapper.'

Henry was still facing the window. 'Someone is trying hard

81

to convince us that they were kidnapped and to link the crime with those of old Joseph Leigh, a hundred and forty odd years ago. But the only material evidence is that parcel of clothes and the cross.'

Judd's pipe was crackling, no other sound to disturb the silence of the room. It was getting dark and Henry went to switch on the lights. 'There's precious little to bite on,' Judd admitted. 'To be frank, I'm not sure where to go from here.'

Henry picked up a little millefiore paperweight and held it so that the refracted light made a pattern on his hand. 'It's just possible that there has been no crime but that someone in the *Peel* household wants us to think there has.'

'What about the cross?'

Henry nodded. 'It presents a problem but not an insurmountable one.'

Judd tapped out the dottle from his pipe into an ashtray. 'It doesn't seem possible! Where could a man hold two girls in secret and against their wills? How could he hold one for that matter?'

Henry put down the paperweight exactly in the middle of a spotless white blotter so that it lay in a spangled halo of light. 'That's the question, isn't it? But Joseph Leigh managed it.'

Judd was contemptuous. 'But that was a hundred and fifty years ago. Things were different—a man was king of his own castle in those days. In any case he had an accomplice in the negro boy.'

The sharp click of the latch of the library door and Flossie was coming down the broad carpeted aisle toward them. She had a remarkable facility for silent movement. The severity of her dress and manner called to mind an old-fashioned district nurse. 'It's the young lady. She telephoned to say that she will be having tea with Mr. Edward and he will be bringing her along to the party this evening.'

Henry thanked her but she continued to stand by the table. 'Would you like your tea now?' The invitation was really a command and needed no reply. 'Perhaps you would like some as well?' She addressed Judd.

82

'No thank you. I must be off but I won't delay Dr. Pym.'

Flossie, her lips pursed, picked up the used ashtray, moved the paperweight back to its accustomed place and withdrew.

There was a good fire in the drawing-room, its leaping flames doing cheerful battle with the gathering darkness, and Mei Mei's decorations looked even more exotic and mysterious high up in the dim flickering light. Henry was alone until Flossie came in with a tray for one.

'Sir Francis is still confined to his room, I'm afraid.' She pulled a small table close to Henry's chair and placed the tray on it. 'Will that suit you, Dr. Pym? Mr. Gerald had to go into town and Miss Lucy—Mrs. North—is gone visiting, so you are alone. Mrs. North was very particular that you should make yourself at home.'

Henry poured his tea while Flossie went to the windows and drew the heavy velvet curtains excluding the night. Then she switched on the chandelier. 'If there is anything you want, Dr. Pym, perhaps you will ring?'

Henry thanked her. He drank two cups of tea and nibbled a semi-sweet biscuit, then he went quietly out of the room and upstairs. He had acquainted himself with the room arrangement and he made for the suite occupied by the Norths. It occupied the whole western side of the house on that floor, opening off a passage which made a 'T' with the main corridor. There were two doors and he knocked at the first—no answer. He turned the knob and let himself into an elegant sitting-room, decorated in the modern style with white painted woodwork, grey walls and a Matthew Smith original, a focus of brilliant colour over the mantlepiece. A bookcase crammed with books on history and philosophy occupied most of one wall, there was a charming little Sheraton writing table in the window embrasure, several wing chairs and a Kirckmann harpsichord. Another of Lucy's talents? A door stood open into a small room, simply furnished, a single bed, a dressing table with a few cosmetic preparations and a built-in wardrobe. Evidently Lucy's bedroom. On the other side of the bedroom a bathroom obviously intended to serve two bedrooms but the communicating door

83

was locked. The tender plant of conjugal felicity must have withered. Henry retraced his steps to the passage. It was characteristic of him that being involved in a case, he felt no compunction in this blatant snooping, he who in ordinary circumstances would have hesitated to glance through an open door into a strange house. He tried the second door off the passage and entered a large room, obviously the one on the other side of the bathroom, but it was a workroom or study with only a divan bed tucked away in one corner to suggest that it was also a bedroom. It was severely functional, the room one would have supposed of a man who was aloof from, perhaps disdainful of indulgence of any sort. A large table placed in a good light, a swivel chair and very little else but bookshelves. And the books were predominantly concerned with China, its history, philosophies, religions and arts. Henry recognized at once that this was no mere random collection of the undiscriminating Sinophile but the library of a scholar. Gerald North must be a considerable figure in Chinese scholarship. From the number of original texts it was obvious that he had acquired some facility with the written language and the only pictures on the walls were framed specimens of calligraphy. On the desk a jar held a variety of brushes and these with a tray of inks suggested that he was himself practised in the art. Also on the desk, a folder, neatly inscribed on the outside, *Illustrations for the Art of the T'ang*. Henry opened the folder, it contained a number of plate-size photographs, all, seemingly, of celebrated museum pieces and each carried on the back a descriptive note with a statement of the provenance of the piece. Several were of lively pottery figurines, two were of wall paintings and one showed a portion of *The Diamond Sutra* scroll. There were two photographs of bronzes—one, which interested Henry especially, of the back of a bronze mirror. It had the traditional scrollwork of intertwined vine leaves round the margin, and a ring of running animals and flying birds around the central boss. To judge from the photograph there was little sign of patination. The note on the back of the photograph gave the diameter of the mirror as 69.5 centimetres but said nothing of its provenance.

84

A clock somewhere in the house chimed and struck five. He had set himself one more task and he could not tell how much time he would have to perform it. He returned to the passage, rejoined the main corridor and stopped outside Sir Francis's room. There was no answer to his knock so he opened the door and switched on the light. The bedroom held no surprises except that it was unoccupied. He crossed to the open door of the bathroom but there was no one there. Sir Francis was not in his room. Either he had made a quick recovery or they had been lying on his behalf.

There was a bookcase beside the bed which drew Henry as a magnet. It contained perhaps sixty or seventy books, the sort of thing a man might stock with his pruned favourites to be read and re-read, the selection of which gives away more of his secrets than a peephole into his bathroom. Henry stooped to examine the titles. A severe lot but predictable if you took Sir Francis seriously, predominantly German authors and of those mainly philosophers and historians. Liebnitz, Kant, Fichte, Schelling, Hegel and, of course, Nietzsche; *Thus Spake Zarathusa* in German and in translation. Henry recalled some of the tremendous aphorisms and wondered: *Man shall be trained for war and woman for the recreation of the warrior: all else is folly*, or *Thou goest to woman? Do not forget thy whip!* or *Man is a rope slung between animal and superman* . . .

Struck by a sudden thought, Henry went quickly through all the titles; then, still not satisfied, removed some of the books in case something had been hidden behind. There was nothing.

'Are you looking for Sir Francis, Dr. Pym?'

Flossie was standing in the doorway. Her manner conveyed neither reproof nor surprise and Henry behaved as though his presence in the bedroom needed no explanation.

'Where is he?'

She shook her head.

'How long has he been gone?'

'Since you and the Superintendent talked to him this morning.'

'The Norths are looking for him?' She was utterly dejected and Henry felt sorry for her. 'This is not the first time, is it?'

'Not by a long chalk!'

'How long does he stay away?'

She shrugged. 'A day or two—once he was gone for over a week; sometimes it's only for a few hours.'

'Women, I suppose?'

She nodded. 'And the drink.' She made a little grimace of distaste. 'There's a place over to Killick—a country club they call it, though I could think of a better name. He always starts from there and he usually ends up with some young piece in one of the hotels.'

'And the official explanation is nettle rash.' He could not keep a trace of amusement from his voice and she smiled.

'Sometimes it's true, he gets terrible attacks, he's had them ever since he was a child.' Henry said nothing and she went on, 'It was no different when his wife was alive, everything smooth and pleasant like for weeks or even months, then all of a sudden he would be off. It's as though every now and then he's got to debase himself—to behave like an animal. Some men are like that.'

'Do they always go to look for him?'

She shook her head with vigour. 'Oh, no, it wouldn't do! They've gone now because you're here and the police and everything . . .' She went over to the bed and straightened the counterpane. 'I mean, what would everybody think if he wasn't here this evening? It's Christmas Day.'

'But surely they haven't much chance of finding him? He could be anywhere.'

'He never goes far afield—ten to fifteen miles at the most and there's not that many places would take him in, knowing what he's up to!'

Henry looked at her drooping figure, all the spirit gone. 'I'm sorry.'

She nodded. 'I've been in this house since I was fourteen—nearly forty years. Sir Francis is the same age as I am and you could almost say we grew up together—allowing for the difference in our situations.'

They were standing in the bedroom and she was facing the swing mirror of the dressing-table. She raised her hand to her hair in an oddly coquettish gesture which made Henry wonder if there had been more between her and Sir Francis than the relationship of employer and employed. Properly dressed and with a hair-do she would have made a good-looking woman and she might well have been a very attractive girl.

'Sir Francis's parents were alive in those days, of course. In fact his younger brother Edward was born just a month before his own daughter, Miss Lucy, and his wife died in childbirth. I had the two babies, uncle and niece with just a month between them, and I was nanny to them both. Then a few years later, when they were growing up, Sir Francis's sister married Harold Vane and her two children, Johnny and Beth, were born and brought up here with only me to look after them. The poor lady herself was took off to the asylum when Beth was only two but long before that she had nothing to do with the children. She would sit, staring at nothing, for hours on end . . . sometimes I would think she'd stopped breathing.'

'A tragic family!'

She sighed. 'They are that! And never did anybody any harm. Always their own worst enemies. Now there's this terrible business about the girls, and people as good as saying it's Sir Francis. Wicked tongues!' She drew herself up and something of her militancy returned, 'Let them say it to me! I don't know what you're really here for, Dr. Pym, but I believe it is to help him. Whether that's so or not, I'll say this: Sir Francis wouldn't hurt a fly—for all his talk.'

Henry made a non-committal but soothing remark and they left the room together. In the hall Flossie moved off toward the kitchen but changed her mind and came back. 'There's one more thing, Dr. Pym. You may be thinking— and the police too for all I know—that a man who carries on like he does might be just the sort to . . . to do something really nasty.' She hesitated and looked at Henry as though she wasn't quite sure whether to go on or not, but she did. 'They say ·

you don't really know what a man is capable of until you've been to bed with him.' Her look was challenging. 'Well, I've been to bed with Sir Francis more times than I could count and I'm not ashamed of it either, though I wouldn't want it talked about for his sake. The point is, I *know* him and for all his talk he wouldn't really hurt a fly.'

Henry went to his room, bathed, changed and sat reading. Christmas dinner had been fixed for eight o'clock but Sir Francis's absence and the consequent disturbance would probably mean a scratch meal and no party afterwards. To judge from the house noises the Norths had returned but he decided that it was better for him to keep out of the way. Shortly after half-past seven he heard Susan moving about in her room next door and he went in. She was undressing and her greeting lacked warmth.

'Am I unwelcome?'

'To hell with that! I'm worried.' She put a hanger through the loops in her skirt band and hung it in the wardrobe. 'It's something that happened while Edward and I were on our way here . . .' She told of the incident in the Willow Garden, while Henry sat on the bed silent and attentive.

'Well? It was unpleasant while it lasted but it's over. You're not usually the sort to worry about things after they've happened. What is it that is really troubling you?'

She slipped into her bathrobe and loosely knotted the belt. 'I didn't see any light in the Mandarin's house.'

'A small hand torch in a building that size doesn't give much light. If somebody was sweeping the beam round you might easily miss the instant when it happened to light up a window.'

She nodded. 'It's possible, of course. In fact, I must have missed it.'

'But you don't think so?'

She really did look worried. 'He said he saw it two or three times.'

'Look at it from another angle then—what would be the point in his pretending? And if there really was no one there it would mean that he smashed the doors himself—why?'

88

'I should have thought that was obvious. By creating the impression that there was someone in the house up to some monkey business he diverts suspicion from himself.' She frowned. 'I hate saying this because I like him and I can't really believe that . . .'

Henry stood up. 'If it's any consolation to you the whole household was on the loose.' He told her about Sir Francis and illogically she seemed to be cheered. Then suddenly she noticed the time and panicked. 'It's a quarter to eight. I shall have to do without a bath!'

The gong sounded promptly at eight but it was ten past before Henry escorted Susan downstairs and in to the drawing-room. They were all there, including, to Henry's astonishment, Sir Francis. He stood on the hearthrug, back to the fire, sherry glass in hand, pale but brimming with hospitality. Edward had told them of the events in the Willow Garden and Susan found herself a heroine. 'But my dear young lady! Are you sure that you feel up to our rather foolish festivities?'—from Sir Francis.

'It was irresponsible of Edward to expose you to such . . . to such a situation! I have always said that the Willow Garden is liable to become a refuge for tramps especially in the winter months'—from Gerald.

Susan protested in vain.

Helen Vane waited until the flutter had died down before saying her piece: 'You and I, my dear, are depressingly secure. The gentleman, it seems, prefers brunettes.'

Lucy was shocked. 'Helen! How can you speak like that? When two young women have been . . . have probably been murdered.'

But Helen was irrepressible. 'If they have it's almost certainly their own fault. In similar circumstances I should act on Lord-Somebody's advice to his daughter, "When rape is inevitable, lie back and enjoy it".'

Edward laughed. 'Good for you, Helen! Always the realist!'

They went in to dinner. Flossie had Sarah to help and Susan was mildly surprised that Sarah's parents were not too scared to let her continue working at the house.

The meal was traditional and even Gerald tasted all the dishes. There were crackers beforehand so that everybody ate wearing an absurd paper hat. The conversation was general and cheerful and for a moment it was possible to be taken in, to believe that here was a family party celebrating Christmas without a care in the world.

Beth Vane was as excited as a child. She was making a bantering attack on her father. 'Are you doing your party piece tonight, dad?'

Harold was quiet, toying with his food and eating little. Now he was brusque. 'You know that I do not like you to speak in that way, Beth.'

'Sorry! But why do you always demonstrate on Helen? Why not me?'

'I don't know if you are a suitable subject.'

'Try me.'

'If you like.'

The English girl's exuberance, her chubby shapelessness, her *naïveté*, contrasted with Mei Mei's self possession, her restraint, and her slim elegance. 'Like a mongrel puppy gambolling round a dignified greyhound,' Susan thought.

'Let him hypnotize you, Mei Mei.'

The Chinese girl patted her lips with her napkin. 'No thank you, I do not want to be hypnotize.'

'*tized* not *tize*.'

Mei Mei smiled. 'All right, I do not want to be hypno*tized*.'

'You're afraid he'll make you tell your secrets—all about you know who.'

'I have no secrets since I tell them to you,' Mei Mei said.

'Can you make people tell secrets they wish to keep?' Beth demanded of her father.

'I think that under certain circumstances it may be possible.'

Mei Mei looked round the table then began to chuckle. 'You should try Uncle Gerald, I expect he has plenty of secrets.'

Harold smiled. 'I don't think he would consent.'

Gerald paused, his water glass half-way to his lips. 'On the contrary, I think it should prove an interesting experiment.'

When the meal was over they toasted each other and absent

friends. Then, in a moment not without pathos, Beth proposed a toast to her brother who, at that moment, was probably roaming round the estate alone, like a rogue wolf. It occurred to Susan that born into a family of another class Johnny would have been closeted and cosseted by the Welfare State, his dependence complete. Here he was treated almost with indifference, his freedom and his individuality thrust back at him. It was very odd.

They moved into the drawing-room and sat about for a while until Lucy became brisk and started to organize them. Then Harold was persuaded to put on his demonstration. A space was cleared in front of the long blue velvet window curtains and a sofa brought into position giving a theatrical air to the proceedings. Beth insisted on being the first subject. After removing her shoes and stockings she lay on the sofa, the chandelier was switched off so that the only light apart from firelight came from a shaded lamp placed on a table near the head of the sofa. Everyone was quiet, the few simple dispositions had created an atmosphere of mystery and expectation. Harold's stocky figure, almost a silhouette against the still form on the couch, became the focus of attention. For a magic moment he was Prospero and Maskelyne, Merlin and Svengali.

'Relax . . . Let your mind go blank . . . Look at this little chain . . . See how it swings . . . Relax. You are feeling drowsy . . . you are going to sleep. I shall count down from ten and when I reach one you will be asleep—deeply asleep. Ten . . . nine . . . eight . . .' He was sitting on the edge of the sofa looking down at his daughter. 'Deeply asleep.'

After a little while he stood up. 'She seems to be a good subject. I am going to try regression in time.' The familiar routine. 'How old are you?' 'I am seventeen.' 'I am going to take you back in time. As I count down the years so you will become younger . . .' Everyone so quiet that the crepitations of the burning logs were painfully intrusive. 'Deeply asleep . . .'

Edward Leigh had found himself a place on a settee next to Susan and his hand came to rest on her knee. She felt the squeezing pressure of his fingers.

'... Eleven ... Ten ... Nine ... How old are you now?'

A voice which sounded distinctly juvenile, 'I am nine years old.'

'What have you been doing today? ... Have you been to school?'

'No, there is no school today ... it is the holidays.'

'What have you been doing?'

Hesitation. 'I went shopping with Flossie.' A short pause then a small flood of words, 'She bought me a present—a book but I couldn't keep it.'

'Why not?'

'Uncle Francis took it. He said I mustn't let Flossie spend her money on me. He was angry and I cried.'

'Why didn't you tell your daddy?'

'Don't be silly. Daddy is in Malaya ...'

Harold carried on with the regression to the Babinsky plantar reflex and back again. At last Beth stood up blinking, feeling slightly foolish and wondering what had happened but pleased because everybody was congratulating her. 'Was I very silly?' ... 'You were sweet!' Susan who had never seen a demonstration of hypnosis before was deeply moved.

'Now I've got some competitions if anybody wants them.' Lucy trying to make sure that nobody had a dull moment.

'What about me? Isn't it my turn now?' Gerald to Harold Vane.

Harold looked at him oddly. 'I didn't take you seriously.'

Gerald smiled, a thin little smile. 'You should, I never make jokes, I don't know how.'

'You surely don't want to be hypnotized, Gerald?' from Sir Francis.

'But I do.'

People had gone back to their places and Gerald took his seat on the settee. 'Do you want me to take my shoes and socks off?'

'I don't think that will be necessary,' Harold said, 'but it might be a good idea to loosen your tie.'

The lights were put out once more and Harold went through

the ritual. It took a little longer but at last Gerald seemed to respond as effectively as Beth had done. 'You are deeply asleep. You feel relaxed?'

'Yes, I feel relaxed.'

'You are contented? Happy?'

'Yes.' Gerald was half-sitting, half-lying across the sofa and he certainly seemed completely and unselfconsciously relaxed.

'May I ask you some questions?'

'Yes.'

'You have a stomach complaint?'

'Yes.'

'And you have to be very careful of your diet?'

'Yes, very careful.'

'Perhaps this evening, because it is Christmas, you have been less so than usual?'

'That is true and I shall pay for it later.'

'No, you will not. When you go to bed tonight you will have an undisturbed night with no pain and no discomfort. In the morning you will wake refreshed. You understand?'

'I understand.'

'Repeat what I have just said to you.'

'When I go to bed . . .' He was almost word perfect.

'What else shall I ask him?' Harold seemed embarrassed.

'May I put one or two questions?' It was Henry.

Harold seemed more than ever put out. 'Dr. Pym wants to ask you some questions, do you agree?'

'Yes.'

Henry walked to the sofa and stood looming over it. 'Mr. North, this is Pym speaking, do you understand what I am saying?'

'I understand.'

'There is something you should tell me is there not?'

'Something I should tell you?'

'Yes, what is it?'

North moved restlessly but did not answer.

'Is it about the missing girls?'

'The missing girls?'

'You know where they are?'

'No.'

'You know who is responsible for their disappearance?'

'No!' Emphatic.

'Is it something about books?'

'I don't know. Perhaps.' The voice was vague, remote, dreamy.

'About one book—a diary?'

'I do not know about a diary.'

An impasse. Henry hesitated and in the silence Gerald spoke without prompting; he spoke like a child about to recite a poem: 'The little lady, of Ch'ing-Hsi.'

'I must wake him.' Harold Vane was concerned, he turned to Gerald and raised his voice. 'I shall count down from five and when I have finished you will wake up quite normally. You will not feel distressed or unhappy . . . Five . . . four . . . three . . .'

Gerald stirred and sat up. A moment later he was standing, a little sheepish. 'Did I make a fool of myself?'

Harold smiled, perhaps relieved. 'Lawyers make tough subjects; they have a built in sales resistance.'

The party broke up just before one and Henry lingered a moment in Susan's room. 'Did you enjoy the party?'

'I was impressed by the hypnotism, I've never seen anything like it before.'

'Little Beth was a good subject.'

'You didn't get much out of Gerald.'

'One never does, he has a devious mind.'

'But under hypnosis . . .'

Henry grinned. 'Hypnosis my foot! He was no more hypnotized than you are and poor Harold knew it, that was why he was so upset.' He moved to the door then turned back. 'By the way, Sir Francis turned up of his own accord, nobody found him. Flossie made an opportunity to tell me during the party.'

'He looked ill.'

Henry grinned. 'Urticaria is a very distressing complaint.'

CHAPTER EIGHT

ANOTHER FINE MORNING, Flossie sweeping back the curtains and letting in a flood of sunshine, Susan blinking herself awake, extricating herself from the toils of a complex dream.

'It's a beautiful morning, miss, but they say on the wireless it's going to thaw. No sign of it yet though.' She brought Susan's tray to the bedside. 'Dr. Pym is up and about already.'

'Unusual for him.'

'He seems a very nice man—understanding. I should think you were very lucky to be working for him.' Henry had the knack of inspiring confidence and even affection in middle-aged and older women. 'I think he'll get to the bottom of this dreadful business if anybody can.'

When Susan went down to breakfast Edward was there. Sarah was shovelling sausages on to his plate.

'Good morning!' He subjected Susan to a close scrutiny. 'You'll pass. I can't stand women who come down to breakfast spotty cheeked, puffy eyed and sullen. You look good enough to eat.'

Susan was still troubled about Edward and in no mood for his flirting. 'It's nice to have your approval and fortunate that you prefer sausages.'

'As a matter of fact I stayed here last night specially to find out.'

Susan asked for a boiled egg and poured herself some coffee while she waited.

'Your boss has gone out but he left you a note.' He pointed to an envelope lying face down by the sugar sifter. Susan opened it.

'Join me when you can at the Mandarin's house but try not to bring your little friend along.'

'A thought for the day?'

'I have to go into town.'

'Don't be silly, the place is clammed up, it's Boxing Day.'

Susan was annoyed. Whenever she told a lie it always back-fired. 'I still have to go.'

'I'll drive you.'

'Thank you but I prefer to drive myself.'

Her egg arrived and she started to trim off the top.

'Are you a virgin?'

'No.'

'That's lucky, I'm scared of virgins.'

'Good for them!'

'Do you mind if I smoke?' He took out the usual packet of crushed cigarettes and lit one. 'I agree with the Prince Regent, taking virginity is a job for labourers.'

'I don't remember having slept with any labourers.'

'Who is or was the little lady of Ch'ing-Hsi?'

'I've no idea.'

'You must admit that was a bloody odd stunt Gerald pulled last night. I mean, it's not like him to put himself on public exhibition.'

'You must know him better than I.'

To her relief Edward made no attempt to follow her when she left the dining-room. She put on boots and a duffle coat and set out across the park for the Willow Garden. The snow was still crisp and there was no wind, the *Pinetum* was criss-crossed by frozen tracks made over three days. The sun was low in the sky and as she came out from the rhodo-dendron thicket on to the slope above the Willow Garden the scene was breathtaking, like a detail from a Ming hand-scroll. Whatever architectural solecisms had been committed in the buildings, however naïve and futile their conception, Joseph had succeeded in creating a landscape which evoked the same nostalgic yearning as the scrolls or paintings on silk. One looked instinctively for the shrouded figures in their broad brimmed hats, their stocky little horses, the half naked coolies with their bamboo shoulder poles and, perhaps, a canvas covered tilt cart bearing some great official with his wives.

Susan found Henry by the damaged doubled doors. He stood, hands thrust deep into the pockets of his overcoat, staring out over the snow. Two lots of footprints reached out about a hundred yards from the building. 'You see the prints?'

'Yes.'

'Two lots.'

'Of course, Edward going and coming back.'

'And the man he was chasing?'

Suddenly Susan felt infinitely depressed. 'So there wasn't anybody.'

'If there was he didn't run this way.'

Susan was silent. A moment or two later she said, 'Henry, do you really thing Edward is mixed up in this?'

His manner was brusque. 'My dear Susan, I'm not clair-voyant! Have you asked him what he was doing in the garage on Christmas Eve night? Was he searching our car?'

'He says not.' And she told him the story of the girl-friend and her handbag.

'Do you believe him?'

'Yes, I do.'

'Then that's your answer, isn't it?' Henry turned abruptly toward the willow tree and the lake, the little timber bridge and the sampans.

> 'Her door opened on the white water
> Close by the side of the timber bridge:
> That's where the little lady lived
> All alone without a lover.'

'The little lady?' Susan asked quickly.

'The little lady of Ch'ing-Hsi. It's a children's song, prob-ably from the fourth or fifth century.'

'So that's what Gerald was trying to tell you! But why on earth couldn't he come straight out with it?'

'Perhaps because he is unable to produce supporting evi-dence. In any case, despite his disclaimer, I suspect Gerald of being quite a joker.'

97

Henry moved off and stood under the great snow laden branches of the willow. 'Couldn't this will-o'-the-wisp of Edward's have got away across the bridge?'

'I don't think so—no, I'm certain he couldn't have, I would have been sure to see him. I was standing almost where you are under the tree.'

Henry walked out on to the floating staging where the sampans were drawn up in two neat rows. He stood for a moment, then beckoned to Susan. The slats were dangerously slippery due to the accumulation of snow on slimy algae. It was only when she stood beside him that she could see the flat-bottomed punt moored to the staging and prisoned in thin ice.

'Have you been to the island?'

'No.'

'Can you punt?'

'No.'

'Then I must. In you get!'

Henry cast off, breaking the ice, and after a few tentative thrusts got into clear water and into the rhythm of the thing so that the craft moved along nicely with the essential watery chuckle coming from under the bows. A pair of mute swans *(Cygnus olor)* came to take a look but sheered off when no food was forthcoming. Half way across the pole lost bottom and Henry all but overbalanced. 'God! You need an Admiralty chart for this!' Certainly the bottom was very variable but by using powerful strokes when he found it Henry was able to span the gulfs with the boat's momentum and they reached the island. It was bigger than it looked from the shore and its banks were protected by a wall of massive irregular stones. There were green and white notices strictly forbidding landing which, in any case, was only possible at one point on the far side of the island where there was a break in the otherwise continuous screen of gorse *(Ulex europaeus)* and goat willow *(Salix caprea)*. Henry scrambled ashore and secured the painter to a thoughtfully provided iron ring and Susan came up after him. They followed a path of untrodden snow encroached upon but not blocked by the gorse and reached a small clearing, a wilderness of weeds; tin cans and a variety of plastic artefacts pushing up through the snow. It was evident that the notices were largely disregarded. Susan looked round with distaste.

'Some people would desecrate paradise.'

Henry grunted. 'Let's hope it will be an extraditable offence.'

Totally screened by the wall of vegetation they were in a circular area perhaps sixty feet in diameter with no view of anything but the sky.

Henry called her and she joined him by a mound of rubble. 'It's a mine shaft and it's open.' The rubble was no more than waist high and they could look down into the shaft for fifteen or twenty feet. The sides of the shaft were of brick in fair condition. Henry lobbed a stone and the splash followed fairly quickly. 'The water's not far down.'

'Probably at the level of the lake.'

'No, it's much deeper than that—a hundred and fifty feet anyway. Very odd!'

'Why is it odd? You said the lake covered some old mine workings.'

'So it does but you wouldn't expect a shaft on top of what is obviously an artificial mound and in any case they wouldn't have bricked up the sides like that.'

Susan sat herself on a boulder. 'Are you thinking that Joseph's secret room might be part of the old mine working.'

'It crossed my mind.'

'And that this is the way in?'

Henry did not answer directly. 'Joseph's room is only of interest if it is being used now for a similar purpose.'

'Well?'

'If it is, then this is not the way in, it's obvious isn't it?'

Susan's face fell. 'Of course, it's out of the question. So we are no further forward.'

Henry shook his head. 'I don't know, we may not have wasted our time.'

He punted them back across the lake and moored the punt

99

where they had found it. They spent the next hour going over the Pavilion and exploring the Mandarin's house. Henry was silent and preoccupied. When Susan spoke he answered in monosyllables. They were standing in the middle of the red tiled floor of the Pavilion when he said, 'You realize that if there is such a room it must be ventilated, it must be lit, and for any extended occupation it would need to be heated. If a girl is to be held a prisoner there she must be fed. It hardly seems possible.'

'But we have found the ventilation shaft—is that it?'

'Perhaps.'

'Then the room is under the lake?'

'It could be.'

Susan shivered. 'Somehow that makes it worse.'

'We are only guessing.'

They walked back arm in arm. Henry had become relaxed and companionable. In the *Pinetum* they stopped to watch the antics of a red squirrel *(Sciurus vulgaris leucourus)* enjoying or enduring one of its brief spells of winter wakefulness. 'In two months' time the males will be fighting for their mates,' Henry observed. 'Which reminds me, how fond are you of that uncouth young man, Edward?'

'Fond is hardly the word. I like him and he is amusing in small doses.'

'But you wouldn't be unduly upset if he happened to break a leg or two in a good cause?'

'Is it likely that he will?'

Henry shrugged. 'It's possible, I am going to suggest that he has a look down that shaft. He seems possessed of a certain simian agility.'

'But I thought that he was high on your list of suspects.'

Henry grinned. 'I wouldn't take that too seriously. He was a victim of the oldest trick in the book. His quarry burst open the doors and doubled back.'

'In that case he's probably expendable,' Susan said, greatly relieved.

The sky which had been clear and blue was darkened by clouds creeping up from the west. The air was distinctly warmer and by the time they reached the house it was moist with the promise of rain. They met Sir Francis in the hall. He was like a man sleep walking, scarcely aware of the world around him, absorbed in an inner life which seemed more real and more disturbing. Susan wondered what could have changed him from the amiable Pickwickian figure who had greeted them on their arrival at *Peel*. In four days.

Henry was brisk. 'We've been looking at the lake and the Willow Garden—a remarkable piece of landscaping.'

Sir Francis smiled vaguely. 'And a remarkable piece of folly! It impoverished the estate for a generation.'

Henry looked sympathetic. 'Did your ancestor, Joseph Leigh plan the work himself or did he employ professional assistance?'

Sir Francis did his best to orientate his thoughts and answer Henry courteously but his mind was elsewhere. 'I think that Joseph was a friend or at least an acquaintance of Sir William Chambers and that he was much influenced by Chambers' writings, particularly his *Designs of Chinese Buildings* and *Oriental Gardens* but I have never heard that Chambers was involved directly. The family account has it that Joseph planned and supervised the work himself and that he imported Welsh miners and Welsh craftsmen to do it.'

'*Welsh* miners?'

Sir Francis nodded. 'Odd, isn't it? When this county's major industry was tin and copper mining. Indeed, the lake itself was made by flooding tin workings which, I understand, were productive at the time.'

Henry expressed interest, thanked Sir Francis and was on the point of continuing into the house when Sir Francis detained him. He spoke in a low voice, 'Pym, I shall be grateful for a private word with you.'

'I'll see if I can find Edward,' Susan said diplomatically.

Henry expected to be taken to the library or the sitting-room, instead Sir Francis led him upstairs to his bedroom. 'I want to show you something.' With a key from his chain he unlocked one of the smaller drawers in a two tiered tallboy and lifted out something swathed in tissue paper which he unwrapped. A pottery figurine covered with blue glaze. He stood it on his dressing-table: a repulsive male figure, naked except for a loin cloth, sprouting wings from the shoulders and having clawed feet, the right hand held a mallet or maul and the left a hafted blade resembling a chisel; a drum hung from his shoulder.

Sir Francis looked at Henry. 'You know something of Chinese *objets d'art*?'

'A little.'

'Then what do you make of this fellow?'

Henry picked up the figure. 'It's rather crude. I've never seen anything quite like it but I don't think that it is particularly old—eighteenth century, perhaps, although it is made in the style of T'ang grave gifts. It's probably from a household shrine.' He stood the figure on the dressing-table once more; its malevolence was disturbing.

'Whom does it represent?' Henry was surprised by Leigh's tone of barely restrained impatience.

'I suppose it's the Taoist Thunder god, My Lord Thunder —Lei-kung. I have never seen him modelled before but he is said to carry a mallet, a chisel and a drum.'

Sir Francis nodded. 'What is the particular function of this god in the Taoist pantheon?'

Henry was mildly resentful of this blatant catechism but assuming that there must be a good reason he answered politely, 'I think it was his job to seek out and punish those who were guilty of a great crime which remained undetected —especially murder.'

Sir Francis was thoughtful. 'That makes sense. I know little about antiques and least of all about Oriental stuff.' He took the figure, rewrapped it in tissue and was about to replace it in the drawer when he changed his mind. 'Look at this!' He had taken from the drawer a .32 automatic pistol. His manner was half sheepish, half defiant. 'You see, I take precautions.'

Henry smiled but said nothing of the pistol. 'About the

figure, has it come into your possession recently?'

Leigh looked at him oddly. 'Yes it has. The night before last was the first time I ever saw it. I woke from sleep and had occasion to switch on my bedside lamp, this thing was staring at me from my bedside table.'

'And you know nothing of its provenance?'

'I told you, I have never seen it before.'

'Have you made any inquiry among members of your household?'

Sir Francis shook his head. 'No, I suspected that it had been put there for a certain purpose and you have proved me right.'

'What are you going to do?'

Leigh made a gesture of helplessness. 'What can I do?'

'You could report this to the police and ask for protection.'

He brushed the suggestion aside. 'You know quite well that there would be no purpose in that.'

'You could lock your door at night and avoid going about the estate alone.'

Sir Francis nodded. 'Yes, I must be more careful, thank you. It is a relief to talk to somebody about it.'

By the time Henry rejoined Susan the rain was coming down steadily washing away the snow in rivers of slush. 'This is better, I hate snow!' Susan had her nose pressed against the window panes like a child. Rain never bothered her and Henry often remarked that she seemed to share an aquatic ancestry with the Cornish who are at their best in a drizzle and are indifferent to a downpour, even if they do not actually enjoy it. 'Edward has gone back to his cottage,' she said over her shoulder.

It was almost twelve and Henry decided to put in an hour on cataloguing the natural history works in the library. 'After all, whatever Leigh's purpose in inviting us here it was for this we accepted.' Susan had a preliminary list of the contents of the chest, now they would start on the books which occupied two bays of the library and comprised over one thousand five hundred books. They had already seen enough to realize that the collection was important and

valuable. But although Susan was an enthusiastic entomo-
logist she could neither emulate nor understand Henry's
ability to detach himself from one problem and apply himself to another. In less than five minutes he seemed to be
immersed in the bibliography of eighteenth-century natural
history, kidnapped girls and secret rooms forgotten.

'Donovan's *Natural History of British Insects* published
in 1799. And look! Here in volume 8—the first record of the
addition of the Chequered Skipper *(Carterocaphalus palae-
mon)* to the British list. We really must devote more time to
this collection, Susan, it's the opportunity of a lifetime.'

Sir Francis and Lucy joined them for lunch but Gerald
was not there. 'He's gone riding,' Sir Francis said. 'It's his
only vice. He keeps a monstrous great bay stallion who
frightens me if I have to get within twenty yards of him.'

'You exaggerate, Father. Jock is as gentle as a lamb.'

Sir Francis laughed. 'All I can say is I'm glad we haven't
any lambs like him in our flock but you stick to your story,
my dear, and I'll stick to mine.'

Susan felt sure that when lunch was over Henry would
return to the library but she was wrong. He told Susan to
bring the car round so that they might call on the Vanes.

The Vane house was on the edge of estate, its garden
fronting on a country lane which pursued a devious way
to join the main road a quarter of a mile away. The house
had once been a farm house, it was large, four-square and
stone built. The walls were covered with ivy and the windows
shone, darkly mysterious. The roof was of Delabole slate,
hipped, gently pitched and overhanging, giving the place a
Queen Anne flavour like the dower house. The garden was
mostly lawn—or field, for there was a general atmosphere
of cosy neglect. Helen Vane received them in a huge sitting-
room furnished with well worn leather armchairs and little
else. The dusty dirty-brown carpet was littered with maga-
zines covering a wide range of dates and dealing with farming
and estate management, on the one hand, and fashion on
the other. Helen disposed herself in one of the chairs. She
wore a very short wrap-over skirt which did not wrap over

enough and did nothing to hide her thighs. She was plaintive.

'I suppose you've come to see Harold? No one comes to see me! Harold has taken the two girls to see some puppies. He's going to buy one for Beth. Anyway they'll be back soon.' She delivered herself of this while she studied her nails with an air of insupportable boredom. 'I suppose it's no good offering you a drink?'

They said that they did not want a drink.

'That affair last night! Wasn't it a drag? Whenever I see the Leighs at close quarters I think they can't be real! Of course Edward is the most presentable but he's odd. I mean, all that talk about sex but when it comes to the point . . . well, I don't think a girl would have to worry too much about Edward. If you ask me, he's queer—literally, I mean . . .'

Fortunately Harold came back with Mei Mei and Beth and though he took Henry off to his office, the girls remained to dilute Helen's gossip. Harold's office was built on to the back of the house. It was full of books, papers, files, maps and photographs. Photographs covered every spare inch of wall, photographs of farm animals decorated with rosettes and looking absurd and of improbable farm buildings under construction. A communicating door into another office stood open and Henry could see two desks with covered typewriters and a telephone switchboard. Harold filled his pipe from a large and ugly silver mounted tobacco jar.

'Farming is a business and farming on this scale is quite a substantial business.' This appeared to be a ritual slogan which he had to get off his chest but did not expect comment on. He lit his pipe and when it was drawing nicely, went on, 'I suppose you've come about that charade last night?'

'Was it a charade?'

Harold shrugged. 'Of course it was—as far as Gerald was concerned—and you must have known it. I was in an impossible position! Gerald is so unpredictable, one moment he is as cold and unresponsive as a glass image, the next you find yourself involved in one of his little hoaxes and he expects you to be amused. He's always been the same.' Harold sat back in his chair, self-confident, expansive, a country squire on his own ground. It was easy to underestimate him in his chosen milieu.

Henry was charming. 'I haven't come to ask you about last night, Mr. Vane, I'm here because your family had the estate before the Leighs.'

The smooth brown patina of Harold's face creased into smiles. 'That was two hundred and thirty-eight years ago, Mr. Pym.'

'All the same, you may be able to help me. Did your family retain any documents connected with the estate?—documents perhaps of sentimental rather than legal importance?'

'I think my ancestors were so hard up they were glad to let their sentiment go with their property. The Leighs took over lock, stock and family portraits—as you have seen for yourself.'

'My interest is in the old mine workings.'

Harold gave him a shrewd look. 'That's different. I may be able to help you there—not because I'm a Vane but, being Cornish and having spent some time in Malaya, I could hardly fail to become interested in tin. I've done a bit of research into the history and prospects of mining in this area.' Harold got up and fetched one of numerous rolls lodged precariously on a shelf. He slipped off an elastic band and unrolled a large scale ordinance survey map of the district, spreading it on his work table. 'There wasn't much in the way of mining in the Vanes' time—just a bit of surface scratching and some streaming. The Leighs cashed in when Wheal Gaddon was opened up for copper at the start of the boom round 1750.' He outlined an area on the map with his pipe stem. 'Here's Gaddon, just up the valley from us. They had to drive an adit to take off their water before they could get deep enough for the copper. This is the line of the adit,' (another line indicated) 'and it goes across our land. Roger Leigh, who must have been a pretty smooth operator, saw his chance, struck a bargain and was able to open up a dry mine. He didn't go deep, he had no need for he was lucky again. He struck carbonas—great masses of granite richly impregnated with tin, each of them as much as thirty yards long, ten wide and about as high. By the turn of the century they were pretty well worked out and there were no more easy pickings so Roger's son, Joseph, closed down, flooded that part of the valley and landscaped it.' Harold lifted his tobacco jar off the map and allowed it to roll up. 'That's how the Leighs have always gone about things. They've known when to move in and when to move out—very few people do.'

Henry was beginning to get the measure of Vane. He was of a type not uncommon in the county at different levels of education and opportunity, born out of due time, steam age technocrats, dinosaurs in the new age of electricity and electronics. It was logical that they should take refuge in agriculture, an industry whose machines remain truly mechanical.

'Are there any maps or plans of the workings?'

Harold shook his head. 'No, but they're simple enough. I've looked out a few documents in the County Record Office and according to them the strike runs due east and west. There is a ventilation shaft still in existence on the island in the lake and the main shaft was probably where the Mandarin's house now stands.'

'These carbonas would now be underground caverns?'

'Yes, gunnises the miners call them.'

'Will they be flooded?'

Harold paused to relight his pipe which had gone out. 'I shouldn't think so. The Wheal Gaddon adit is still effective as far as I know and if the lake water got into the workings it would drain away through the adit and empty the lake, the stream wouldn't keep pace with it.'

Henry was impressed by his objectivity. He must know that the questions did not spring merely from an interest in industrial archaeology and he was too intelligent not to link them with the legend of Joseph's room on the one hand and the missing girls on the other, yet he gave no sign.

He must realize that if the crimes were centred on the estate he was an eligible suspect. Marriage to a magazine illustration must bristle with frustrations, he was at what is called the dangerous age, he knew the estate better than anyone else and here he was admitting to specialist knowledge of the mine workings.

Harold's was a massive personality; Henry could think of no other apt description. He dominated this untidy old-fashioned office, it almost seemed part of him, an extension of his personality. He was unflappable, probably also implacable in any cause he felt drawn to. But was he a sadist? Henry thought not. But he was a lusty man and like many super males he might have a contempt for women, hold them cheap, perhaps expendable.

The rain hammered on the flat roof and streamed down the window panes. Although it was only three o'clock it was almost dark. Harold got up and switched on the light. As he sat down again he faced Henry with a faint smile, 'Do you ever take advice, Dr. Pym?'

'Rarely.'

'In this case you would be wise to make an exception. Leave this investigation to the police.' He held up his hand when Henry would have spoken. 'Don't mistake me; I understand that you have a reputation, probably well deserved, for your work with the police but here you are dealing with a very strange family. The missing girls have nothing to do with *Peel*, of that I am quite sure.'

'I hope that you are right but if you are there is a good deal to explain.'

Harold nodded. 'You are thinking of the anonymous letters, the missing pages from Roger's diary, the fact that the pages turned up in Gerald's handkerchief box—but you must have seen enough of police work to know that every major case brings its crop of eye-witnesses who weren't there, false confessions, false accusations—all from kinks.' He sat back in his chair and spoke with great seriousness, 'Believe me, Dr. Pym, at *Peel* we have more than our share of kinks.'

Henry noted the significant omissions from Harold's list

108

of things which linked *Peel* with the girls but he said nothing and Harold went on, 'But I don't think we have any kidnappers, murderers or sadists and I would have thought the old Tudor mansion, long demolished, a far more likely site for Joseph's room than a disused mine working.'

Henry never took kindly to instruction and now he drew the line firmly, 'What you say is very reassuring and I agree with a good deal of it but the main purpose of my visit was to ask if you can provide from the estate yard, say, fifty fathoms of good rope, a bosun's chair and a tripod and pulley device?'

Harold accepted the snub with good grace. 'For the ventilation shaft?'

'Yes.'

'We could manage that. Who is to be your adventurer?'

'I propose to ask Mr. Edward Leigh.'

Harold raised his eyebrows. 'Technically, a very good choice. He has done a lot of pot-holing in the past.'

'So I understand.' Henry stood up. 'Very well, Mr. Vane, I am grateful for your co-operation.'

When they were leaving the rain had eased and Mei Mei and Beth came with them to the car. 'Shall we be seeing you both this evening?' Susan trying to say the right thing.

Mei Mei made a wry face. 'Not me. I am a working girl and I am on night duty, start eight o'clock.'

'What about you, Beth?'

'We're going to a party.' She did nothing to hide the fact that it was not a party she was looking forward to. 'Some friends of Helen's at Penzance have invited us and we shall be staying overnight.'

With an interruption for their meal, Henry and Susan worked all the evening in the library and went to bed weary.

CHAPTER NINE

THE LONG WARD almost silent, settling down for the night, most of the men still sitting up, some of them reading, some listening to the wireless through earphones, some simply staring into space. Wong Mei Mei—Nurse Wong—prim in her uniform, sitting at her little table entering reports. The main ward lights were off and the shaded bed-head lamps made small bright pools which just failed to overlap and left narrow corridors of darkness between one bed and the next. Mei Mei wrote within her own isolating circle of brilliance. Night Sister Martin came in through the swing doors and stood beside her.

'All in order, nurse?' Whisper.

'Yes thank you, sister.'

'Had a good Christmas?'

Mei Mei laughed silently. 'Such as it was, one day off now I do night duty!'

Sister Martin nodded. 'I know. That's nursing! Why do we do it?' She drew up a chair and settled down for a few minutes' gossip. She liked the little Chinese girl and, to tell the truth, she was curious about *Peel*. But a telephone rang remotely. 'Damn! I've a feeling it's going to be one of those nights.' She hurried out into the corridor and into the little box that was her office where the telephone was shrilling in rhythmic bursts. She picked up the receiver. 'Night sister here.'

The porter's voice: 'Outside call for you, sister.'

Then another man's voice, cultured, accustomed to deference. 'This is Mr. Gerald North of *Peel Place*. Are you the night sister in charge of the male wards?'

'Yes, Mr. North.'

'I want you to give a message to Nurse Wong—*Nurse Wong*—can you hear me?'

'Perfectly, Mr. North.'

'I want you to tell her that there is a cable from her people in Malaya—an urgent cable which requires her immediate attention. Try not to alarm her but the matter is urgent. Tell her that if she starts walking either Sir Francis or I will come to meet her with the car.' A pause, then: 'I expect this is inconvenient for you, sister, but I assure you that it is necessary.'

Sister Martin would have liked to point out that it was rather more than inconvenient but she had a soft spot for Mei Mei and she was impressed by North who among other things was chairman of the Board of Management. 'Very good, Mr. North.'

'Thank you, sister.' A click and the ringing tone.

'The old . . . What does he think a hospital is?'

'It will be bad news of my father.' Mei Mei looked grave. 'For six months he has been receiving treatment for pulmonary tuberculosis, then in her last letter my mother say he has pneumonia and is very ill . . .'

'But there is nothing you can do tonight.'

She shook her head a little hopelessly. 'But I must go and see . . .'

Sister Martin patted her shoulder kindly. 'Of course you must, my dear. We shall manage here. And try not to worry, it may not be as bad as you think. You run along and change.'

Ten minutes later a forlorn little figure in a green mackintosh, with a shoulder bag hanging at her hip, stepped out from the brilliantly lit vestibule into the forecourt. The rain had stopped but the wet tarmac gleamed with reflected ribbons of light. It was little more than a mile from the hospital to the gates of *Peel*, with street lamps most of the way, for the town had thrust out a straggling suburb almost to the boundary of the estate. Mei Mei walked quickly, keeping an eye open for approaching cars but preoccupied by speculation about the news that awaited her in the cable. Almost certainly it would mean that within forty-eight hours she would be flying home, and what then? Scarcely noticing, she had reached the end of the street lamps, the last of the villas each with one or two rectangles of orange light, the end of the pavement. Now she was walking by the high stone wall which surrounded the estate, soon she would be at the gates and the lodge. She hoped that the car would meet her by then for she dreaded the prospect of the long walk through the estate in pitch darkness. And it was dark —very dark. Looking up she could see no stars, only the faintest luminosity, a blueing of the blackness with a fine tracery of elm twigs etched against it. An owl hooted close by. A very long way away the lights of a car flickered in and out among the trees but it was travelling on the road beyond the gates of *Peel*. She reached the gates just as the car swished past in a tearing blaze of light so that the way through the estate seemed blacker still. And there was no light in the lodge; Simmonds must have gone to bed. If he had been up she might have waited there. She listened: no sound of a car, so she set out.

'Mei Mei is missing.' The words filtered through into Susan's sleep to become part of her dream, disturbing, frightening. She shifted restlessly and opened her eyes.

'Mei Mei is missing.' Henry was bending over her and it was broad daylight. Then she remembered. After a disturbed night Flossie had brought her tea but she must have fallen asleep again for the tea remained untouched on her bedside table. She remembered too that Mei Mei had said she would be on night duty.

'When she didn't arrive home at her usual time this morning Harold rang the hospital and they told him that Gerald North had telephoned the night sister at a little after ten last night to say that there was an urgent cable for Mei Mei from her people in Malaya and that he wanted her released from her duties immediately. He promised that either he or Sir Francis would come to meet her with the car.'

Susan was still making the adjustment between dream and reality. 'I don't understand. What went wrong?'

'There was no cable, it was a pretext.'

'And they let her go?'

'Why shouldn't they? Apart from anything else Gerald is chairman of their Board of Management.'

'But it couldn't have been Gerald. What does he say about it?' She realized that she was being dense but she could not grasp what had happened.

Henry looked grave. 'It was Gerald but he had the message from Sir Francis and nobody has seen Sir Francis since he went to meet Mei Mei.'

'You mean he's disappeared too?' She felt empty inside. Mei Mei. It was one thing to hear of the kidnapping and probable murder of girls you had never seen but little Mei Mei . . .

Henry was brisk. 'You'd better get up, Susan, we shall need the car. Judd is on his way and Harold is getting together the gear to investigate the ventilation shaft.'

Susan got out of bed obediently but still bemused. 'Surely Sir Francis wouldn't have been so open about it if . . .'

Henry was standing looking out of the window, his back to her. 'We've got to find the girl before it is too late.'

When Superintendent Judd arrived he first interviewed Gerald North, then Henry took him to the library. Susan noticed that Henry now behaved almost as though he were in his own home, certainly with none of the diffidence of a guest.

Judd sat by one of the windows staring out at a small sector of sodden grass bounded by a wall of pale grey mist. He polished his spectacles. 'Well, I suppose this settles it. But I still can't credit that there is some sort of secret hideout under the lake, it's too fantastic.'

Henry was as edgy and ill-tempered as Susan had ever seen him. 'Have you any suggestion of your own as to where we might look?'

The Superintendent shook his head. 'No specific suggestions—no.'

'Then there is nothing to be lost in following up mine. Not that I am asking for police assistance.'

Judd was unimpressed. 'I'm not happy with your ideas in this case, Henry. You may be right but I don't like having all our eggs in one basket. It could still be that these disappearances have no direct connection with *Peel*. Sir Francis, for example, might be off on another of his little sprees. We're jumping to conclusions.'

'So?'

Judd fiddled with his moustache. 'I should be criminally negligent if I failed to start a full-scale routine search for the girl.'

'Then why don't you?'

'I have. My chaps are organizing it at this moment. They have instructions to cover as much ground as they can within a five mile radius of the hospital—woods, commons, waste ground—the usual—*including this estate*.' He smiled. 'Who knows? They might stumble on the Open Sesame for your underground cavern or whatever it is.'

'Good. What do you expect me to say? That you are a diligent policeman following routine?'

Judd made no direct reply but he looked relieved. 'I've also arranged for all stations to be notified and for a request for information to be broadcast on radio and television—not that I have much hope there; I agree with you, this is a local affair.'

Henry was disinterested. 'More to the point: I suppose your searchers will keep in touch by wireless?'

Judd looked surprised. 'Of course, why?'

'I want you to station a constable with a radio at the lake so that we can get help quickly if we need it.'

The Superintendent smiled. 'Fair enough.'

Henry was thoughtful. 'I think I would like to talk to Gerald.'

The Superintendent grinned. 'You're welcome.'

When Judd had gone Henry sent Susan in search of Flossie and the whereabouts of the Norths. According to Flossie they were still in their rooms so Henry led the way upstairs but on the landing instead of making for the Norths' suite he went to Sir Francis's door. He knocked and, receiving no reply, went in. Susan followed, feeling like a thief. The bed was undisturbed, already the room had an untenanted look.

Henry pointed to the bookcase. 'Go through those books, Susan.'

'What am I supposed to be looking for?'

'You'll know if you find it.' Henry at his most provoking but she was relieved; from past experience she knew that this sort of showmanship meant that he had picked up the end of the thread—or thought he had. She knelt on the carpet and began to examine the books. Henry turned his attention to the tallboy and with a pick-lock succeeded in opening the small drawer in which Sir Francis had placed the little figurine of Lei-kung. But it was not there, only the tissue in which it had been wrapped. The gun, too, was missing. Far from disappointing him the absence of the figure and the gun seemed to give him satisfaction and as he closed and relocked the drawer he hummed a little tune. Like a cat fed on cream, Susan thought.

'Found anything?' He moved to stand over her.

'Nothing but some pretty heavy bedside reading.'

'You've been through them all?'

'I have.'

'Then pull them out and look behind.'

She lifted the books from the top shelf—nothing; the same with the second, but the removal of books from the third shelf brought to light a heavy volume placed flat against the back of the case. 'It's the diary!'

Henry nodded with satisfaction. 'I told you that you would know when you found it.' He started to put the books back in the shelves. 'It may be that we are ahead of his time-table so let's leave them as though they hadn't been disturbed.'

When all the books were back in place Henry stole out into the corridor with exaggerated caution before he would allow Susan, carrying the diary, to follow him. 'Your room, it's closer.'

Once in Susan's room he locked the door, switched on the electric fire and drew up two chairs, then he settled down, taking the book on his lap. He flicked through the pages until he came to the year 1828, then he proceeded more slowly. 'Most days are dismissed in a line or two, many days

are not entered at all—here's quite a screed—no, these are
his observations on *The Voices of Fish*—interesting to read
later.' He continued to turn the pages. 'Here's something!'
He smoothed the page and read aloud:

'August 27th. Wednesday.
Pursuant to my firm resolve to discover if there be any
truth in the accusations which are daily levelled against
my father I have of late kept close watch upon his movements and, on the pretext of my concern for his failing
health, I have engaged Roscrow, my valet, to do likewise.
For some weeks my vigilance furnished me with no more
evidence than would confirm me in my filial regard, until
one evening, after my father had ostensibly retired to his
room, I saw him walking near the Willow Garden. I would
have given the matter little thought, supposing that he
had found himself disinclined for rest, had he not, when
I presented myself, manifested anger and chagrin in the
greatest degree possible, accusing me of spying and of
other things not fit to be mentioned. My fears and sus-
picions being thus revived I redoubled my surveillance
and after seven nights I reaped my reward. From my
vantage point in the attic room whence I am able to keep
a great part of the estate in view at once, I saw him set
forth, at least an hour after he had made the pretence of
retiring for the night. I made haste to follow and succeeded in getting and keeping near to him without difficulty
for his route lay along the margins of the trees which,
whilst they afforded him some cover did a like service
for myself.
I was in no doubt that he was bound for the Willow Garden
and so it proved though not as I supposed for either the
Pavilion or the Mandarin's house. On the slopes above
the lake where he has recently established a plantation of
the new Turkey Rose Bay I was forced to fall further
back and it was at some distance that I observed him
to enter the garden of the Pavilion and to begin a circuit
of the building. Suddenly he stopped short near the orna-

mental balustrade and assumed a crouching position which he maintained for a full minute, then he disappeared! Darkness was coming on apace and at first I supposed that I had been a victim of some optical phenomenon but when I approached the place where I had last seen him, having it in my full view the whole time, he was still nowhere to be seen and neither was there any evidence of how his disappearance might have been contrived. What with this mystery, the approach of the night, the eerie aspect of the place and the legend of the miners buried alive whose cries, it is said, may sometimes be heard, I had no stomach to persevere further with my quest and so, resolving to return at a more seasonable time, I set out for home.

Yet one more incident served to disturb me before I reached there. On my way through the trees, it being now almost dark, hearing heavy footfalls approaching, I drew to one side so that I might see without being seen, and who should it be but Jeremiah the black, proceeding at a great pace, carrying some burden, his eyes staring ahead and seeming to shine in the darkness. I made no move to stay him for I felt a certain fear, and it being in any case, unprofitable to question a deaf mute I made my way safely home.'

Henry stopped reading and drew a deep breath. Susan who had been sitting forward in her chair, staring at the electric fire, straightened abruptly. 'Is that all?'

'No, there's more.' Henry shifted his position and resumed reading:

'August 28th. Thursday.
Though my eyes were near to closing with sleep I watched for my father's return until after three and had the satisfaction of seeing him and the black enter the house together, then I went to bed.
It happened that the next day my father had a project to visit a cousin at Landreath so that he would be absent

the whole day and despite the lateness of his return he was early abroad and by seven in the morning he and Jeremiah were away with the coach to Bodmin. The weather which had been very fine these many days suddenly broke and a drizzle of rain spoiled what little pleasure I might have taken in the prospect of the day. However I set out within a few minutes of eight o'clock. Because of my intention that no one shall penetrate to to the evil and secret place of my father's contrivance, I shall refrain from describing the mechanism of entry. Suffice it to say that I spent three hours on the very spot from which he had disappeared before I stumbled on the secret, which, when it is known, appears very elegant and simple though it cost me a sadly sprained ankle in the discovery.

I found myself on a landing of a spiral stone staircase which continued on downwards into darkness. Before closing the entrance (which, I may say, is easily accomplished from below) I lit the lantern with which I had come provided. The descent was easy though long for I counted above one hundred and fifty steps and these delivered me into a commodious tunnel or passage in which the downward slope continued very gently for fifty paces. I knew that I must now be under the lake though the dryness of the walls and the freshness of the air served to mitigate the concern I might have felt on this score.

I was confronted by a heavy oaken door provided with a latch of iron such as are found in churches. I lifted the latch scarce knowing whether I would have it yield or no but the door opened easily and silently and the light of my lantern showed me a sight the like of which I never expected to see in my life. I was entering what I take to be a reconstruction of the salon or living quarters of a wealthy Chinese gentleman of taste although I have no knowledge of these things and little patience with the fashion which in past years so over rated the arts and culture of that nation. Nevertheless I could but gaze about me with admiration and astonishment; at the richness of the tapestries,

at the glowing colours of the lacquer, at the delicate objects
of porcelain and jade, at the curious and elegant works in
metal, some of which I supposed to be merely decorative
while others seemed to have uses such as to accommodate
a lamp or candle, and one, an elaborately worked metal
pan standing on iron legs, to hold charcoal for a fire which
it did and was furnished with a copper canopy suspended
over it and a pipe to take the fumes away.

The chamber was large and lofty so that the light from my
poor lantern revealed only a fraction at a time as I advanced
slowly and a little fearfully over the rich carpet but at the
far end I came upon a lacquered screen consisting of many
hinged panels enclosing a bed or divan, low, and spread with
cushions and having two gowns of the finest embroidered
silk laid upon it.

I marvelled not only at these wonders themselves but more,
if it be possible, that it was my father who had gathered
them together and contrived their accommodation; all this
when even to imagine him in such a setting is utterly beyond
my powers! I begin to understand why it was that he so
persuaded me to prolong my sojourn abroad in the years
which saw the turn of the century when all this was in the
doing. I see too the explanation of a mystery which puzzled
me greatly on my return and about which my father could
by no means be persuaded to speak. That is to say the
disappearance from the house of the many rich gifts which
were made to my grandfather for his services to the Turkish
Porte, such as carpets and tapestries and pottery and metal
vessels of every description. But all these I now perceive
have been incorporated in my father's great design.

Had I gone no further I would have come away ashamed
and with a greater respect for my father's taste and resource
though mystified by his excessive secrecy, but God willed it
otherwise.

By the screen I perceived, almost hidden by the hangings,
a small door which opened to my touch and led me into the
place which has confirmed my worst fears and caused me
to see in him, as I now do, the incarnation of Evil. The

room I entered was as bare as the other was luxurious, a stone chamber of no great size, and so, sufficiently illumined by the light of my lantern to enable me to take in all at once. And what I saw will remain with me until I die. The furnishing was simple: a wooden bench with instruments of torture, thumbscrews, branding irons and worse; a brazier, and, against one wall, a rack of whips of great variety from a light carriage whip to heavy plaited thongs of raw hide. But these things I observed later, what caught and held my gaze, fascinating and revolting me, was the figure of a girl suspended by her hair from a hook in the ceiling so that her feet just trailed the floor. She had . . . But I cannot bring myself to write of what had been done to her, suffice it to say that she was mercifully dead. Of that I steeled myself to make sure.

Now it is past midnight yet I cannot sleep and I write this both to ease my mind and so that it may be a constant rebuke to me if, like Hamlet, I find myself tardy in doing that which I know must be done.'

Henry closed the book.

Susan stood up, white faced. 'We are wasting time, Henry. We must find the way in.'

He took her hand, gently. 'I know how you feel, Susan, but we should never succeed. Knowing exactly where to look— which we do not—Roger Leigh took three hours to find it. No! Harold Vane is organizing men from the estate and equipment, Edward is an experienced pot-holer. I am convinced that they will get in through the ventilation shaft. In any case, it's the best chance we have.'

Susan's voice was brittle. 'If you are right, if it is a ventilation shaft!'

He turned on her angrily. 'Yes, if I am right! You are not the only one who is anxious, Susan.'

'I'm sorry.'

He put his arm round her shoulders. 'No need to be. Go along to the lake and use that woman's tongue of yours to get them moving.'

'You're not coming?'

'Later. There is something I have to do first.'

As Susan reached the door he called her back. 'Again, if I am right, we shall find that Roger's story was not a blue-print for what has happened to these girls.'

When Susan was gone he picked up the diary and went along the passage to the Norths' suite. Outside the sitting-room door he paused; someone was playing the harpsichord, a Chopin *scherzo* played with great skill. He knocked but it was only at his third attempt that the tumbling river of sound ceased abruptly and Lucy North came to the door. She was pale with dark rings below her eyes.

'Come in, Dr. Pym, I'm sorry if I have kept you waiting.' She nodded toward the harpsichord, 'One has to do something, I hope that it doesn't make me seem to be insensitive.'

Henry made reassuring noises but she continued to justify herself. 'He is my father, Dr. Pym, and even if I was in a position to help I could not. We are all victims of our heredity and it is hard to know where the guilt lies.'

She sat him in one of the wing chairs and offered him a cigarette from a silver box. When he refused she took and lit one herself, clumsily, as though smoking was an unaccustomed indulgence. Henry disposed himself comfortably but Lucy remained standing, her agitation would allow her no rest. She screwed up her eyes against the smoke which she was too inexpert to control. 'You understand now what I meant when I spoke to you of the taint.'

' "Hard to know where the guilt lies." ' Strange words! And as he repeated them she looked at him almost fearfully.

'Perhaps I do not want to know.'

He spoke gravely. 'I see that you have thought about it a great deal, perhaps you have also discussed it with your husband?'

She caressed her throat with her fingers, probably to relieve an hysterical constriction. 'No, Gerald and I were not in each other's confidence, we do not discuss things.'

Henry was puzzled by this woman who had cast herself in the colourless role of affectionate daughter and dutiful wife, apparently striving to repress every scrap of the vitality and creativeness that was in her. His words were not explicitly relevant but she replied at once to their implication when he said, 'You married Mr. North.'

'Yes. I married him because he is undemanding and considerate, he is one of us and I thought that between us we could keep an eye on things here.' She crushed out her cigarette, one third smoked. 'It hasn't worked.'

'Why not?'

She perched herself on the edge of a chair. 'At first Gerald and my father got on well enough but it didn't last. Father has an unfortunate knack of finding other people's weaknesses and playing on them; Gerald is sensitive and the combination brought intolerable tension.' She hesitated then added, 'In all fairness I must admit that the fault was not Gerald's.' She was staring blankly, perhaps living again through a catalogue of petty incidents which had demeaned their relationships. 'Sometimes I wonder how he can put up with it.'

Henry maintained a sympathetic silence before changing the subject. 'Mrs. North, does your father have any knowledge of oriental *objets d'art*?'

She smiled, transforming her countenance. 'Daddy? He is a dyed-in-the-wool Philistine where art is concerned, oriental or otherwise.'

Henry thanked her. 'Now, if I may, I should like to talk to your husband.'

She looked startled. 'Gerald? I expect that he is in his room —probably worrying away at his translations—we each have our own preferred opiate.'

Henry wondered whether she would try to cover the fact that there was no communication between the rooms but to his surprise she went to a wall cupboard and lifted a telephone receiver. 'Gerald? . . . Dr. Pym is here and he would like a word with you . . . No, that should be all right.' She dropped the receiver and turned to Henry. 'Do you mind going along to his room? It's the next door down the corridor.'

'Come in!'

Gerald North did not bother to get up; he was seated at

his desk and wearing a pair of heavy library glasses which accentuated the skull-like character of his head; the skin seemed to be drawn tight over the bone. He, too, looked weary and ill. He waved Henry to a chair. 'You are with us at a very sad and distressing time, Dr. Pym.'

'Which is not entirely a coincidence.'

North looked at him over his glasses. 'No, I take your point. I must confess that it was I who persuaded Francis to write to invite you. I knew that the library material would be of interest to you and I hoped that your presence here might . . .' His voice trailed off.

'Might what, Mr. North?'

'Might have . . . stabilized the situation.'

'Is that all?'

North removed his glasses and stared out of the window. 'No, you are right, of course. I had a certain idea which seemed so incredible, so fantastic, that I could not trust my own judgment, I needed someone from outside, someone un-biased and someone with experience . . .' He turned to face Henry and a smile flickered momentarily over his lips. 'You fitted the bill.'

'But Sir Francis admitted to me that the primary reason for my being here was connected with the accusations which were being made against the family.'

'Oh yes, I made no secret of that.' Gerald played with his glasses for a moment. 'This is extremely difficult and painful for me, Dr. Pym, events have reached a crisis which I have foreseen and dreaded . . .' He shifted abruptly, almost irritably in his chair. 'With your experience you will be well aware that such people have an abnormal conceit—that they are psycho-pathic egoists—*nothing* can touch them.'

'Sir Francis represented to me that he himself was in danger.'

North shrugged. 'I don't think that you need me to comment on that.'

Henry nodded. 'This idea of yours which seemed so fantastic, was it supported by evidence—before today, I mean?'

'Evidence?' Gerald considered. 'Circumstantial evidence,

certainly. Periods of absence coincided with certain events; there were suggestive circumstances connected with the anonymous letters—they contained information which, it seemed, could have come only from one source . . .' He paused then added, 'A number of things which, taken together . . .'

'You knew about the mine?'

Gerald was speaking slowly, haltingly, almost like a man under the influence of drugs, as though he needed every effort of will to formulate answers to the questions which were put. Alternatively it could have been that he was profoundly preoccupied, that the conversation only engaged the superficial levels of his mind. 'I knew of the existence of the mine workings under the lake, of course.'

'And you suspected that they might have been the venue for Joseph Leigh's debauchery and for . . .'

'The possibility occurred to me. I could think of no other feasible location. The more I thought of it the more likely it seemed. I have a high regard for Joseph's intelligence and I have always found it difficult to reconcile this with those stage properties which he erected by the lake, they are unworthy of him, no more than illustrations for a child's fairy story. It seemed logical to me to suppose that they were cover for an undertaking of greater significance which, for some reason, he wished to keep secret.'

'And you chose to convey your idea to me through the little lady of Ch'ing-Hsi?'

Another ghost of a smile and no reply.

'Thank you, you have been very helpful.'

Gerald's eyes rested on the diary which Henry still carried under his arm. 'You found it, then?'

Henry nodded.

'Where?'

It was Henry's turn to smile and say nothing.

'By the way, Mr. North, do you know of a pottery figurine representing the Taoist Thunder God?'

Gerald looked surprised. 'Lei-kung? No, I do not, I cannot recall having seen such a thing. Why?'

Again Henry was silent. North was uneasy, he glanced

significantly at the diary. 'I understand that you are going to try the shaft on the island?'

'It seems our best hope.'

The lawyer nodded. 'Unless the diary suggests some alternative.'

'The diary merely confirms what we already suspected, that Joseph had rooms constructed under the lake in the old workings.'

North traced complex patterns with his fingers on the blotting pad. 'Superintendent Judd came to see me this morning; he seemed to suggest that I was in some measure to blame for what has happened to Mei Mei.'

'Indeed?'

'On reflection, I can sympathize with his point of view and I am distressed about it. Although my suspicion had been aroused I fell in with Francis' scheme and allowed myself to be persuaded to telephone the hospital. All I can say is that his account of the cable was so circumstantial that it never occurred to me to doubt it. They had telephoned from the Vanes', he said, asking one of us to get in touch with the hospital and, if possible, to fetch Mei Mei. This seemed reasonable as Helen had gone off with their car and the estate transport is garaged a good mile from their house.' He broke off with a little helpless gesture. 'It is easy to reach a conclusion on logical grounds but it is a different matter to accept the idea that someone whom you have lived with for many years is . . .'

Henry nodded. 'Yes, I can understand that. The Superintendent is particularly distressed about these girls—partly, I think, because he has a daughter of his own.' Henry stood up to go.

'If I can be of any help, Dr. Pym . . .'

'Thank you, I will keep in touch.'

CHAPTER TEN

IT WAS HALF past ten when Henry left the house and set out for the lake. He had to walk, and he stepped out as briskly as he could over the sodden grass. The rain had stopped and a pearly luminosity promised sun behind the slowly thinning mist. No one to be seen, not a sound. Through the *Pinetum*, the trees dripping, down the rhododendron slope and out on to the grass above the lake. From about here Roger Leigh had watched his father operating the mechanism which admitted him to his secret rooms.

'I observed him to enter the garden of the Pavilion and to begin a circuit of the buildings. Suddenly he stopped short, near the ornamental balustrade . . .' Which could mean anywhere along almost a hundred yards of stone wall. And how near is near?

Not that Henry could see any of it now for the roofs of the Pavilion and of the Mandarin's house loomed insubstantially, seeming to float above the mist which was still thick over the lake.

He arrived on the landing stage thinking that he might have to launch one of the ridiculous sampans and paddle himself across but the punt was there. He stepped into it and was about to pole off when Johnny came lumbering up. His pale blue overalls were darkened by the damp, beadlets of moisture stood out on his woollen pullover, his hair hung lank and his face shone but he was grinning and gesturing, apparently happy. Henry had little option but to take him in the punt and he sat in the stern quiet as a mouse.

A few lengths from the shore and they were isolated in a circle of brown water which rippled and chuckled past their bows but it was not long before the island was in sight and Henry was able to punt round to the landing place. A beamy rowing boat, black and businesslike, was tied to the iron ring and Henry moored beside it. He could hear voices now and the clink of metal on metal. Johnny hopped ashore with surprising agility and disappeared along the path to the clearing.

The clearing was transformed and populous. A tripod shear-legs spanned the shaft, its legs bedded in the rubble; a pulley block was slung from the legs and the rope carried back over a two-handed winch which had been staked down a matter of ten or twelve feet away. Harold Vane and one of his work-men were fastening the bosun's chair to the pulley block while three other estate men stood by smoking. Susan was there, Edward and Johnny apparently trying to communicate in earnest dumbshow and, standing a little apart, Judd's constable with his radio peeping above his top jacket button.

'Can you get into touch with headquarters with that thing?'

'Not directly, sir, but radio cars are patrolling the search area and I can report through them.'

'You've checked?'

'Oh, yes, sir.'

Edward wore a waterproof tunic and trousers and heavy boots. He carried a helmet with a torch strapped above the brim like a miner. He seemed to be having difficulty with Johnny who was becoming more and more excited but he raised his hand to Henry in mock salute, 'Just in time for the launching.'

'Ready when you are, Edward.' Harold was standing on the edge of the shaft, his body braced against one leg of the tri-pod, holding the chair. Edward eluded Johnny and stepped lightly over the rubble on to the chair; as it swayed pendulum fashion, he slid down to a sitting position. Harold steadied it. 'O.K.?'

Edward grinned. 'Lower away!'

The four estate men manned the winch, two to each handle and the ratchet began to click slowly as they paid out rope. 'Say when.' Harold called and Edward's voice, already hollow and echoing came up in full song.

'Don't go down in the mine, daddy,
Something will happen today!'

Susan shrugged with irritation and Henry saw it, 'Don't be too hard on him.'

For once, Johnny's smile was gone, he looked sad and disconsolate.

'Twenty-five feet, Mr. Vane.' From one of the winch men. No noise but the click of the ratchet, the pulley and the winch were silenced by grease.

'All right, Edward?'

'A picnic. It's bricked up all the way down, as far as I can see. We should do this more often.'

Susan wondered what it was they were all expecting to find. What did she expect? She had a vague notion of a tunnel going off from the shaft part way down. What else could there be? But perhaps the tunnel would be too small for a man. Perhaps there would be no tunnel, perhaps it wasn't a ventilation shaft after all. How could they be so calm? So lighthearted? Perhaps she would feel better if she was doing something; she felt so helpless.

'Fifty feet, Mr. Vane.'

The rope swung a little but not much, Edward had a short pole to fend himself off and he must be doing it quite skilfully.

'What's the air like?'

Susan did not hear the distorted words. 'What did he say?' Harold grinned. 'Edward is just being Edward.'

Just after the man had called a hundred and twenty-five feet, a shout from below brought the winch to a halt.

'Found something?'

An unintelligible reply.

'You don't need to shout. Speak normally.' Harold instructed and to Susan's surprise Edward's voice came up quietly conversational and perfectly clear.

'There's an opening but it's been built up with chequered brickwork—just a single course it seems to be . . . Yes it is. I can see through the spaces into a passage. The passage looks plenty big enough—three foot six to four foot high . . . and it seems dry.'

'Can you see anything below you?'

A pause, then: 'The shaft goes on down a good bit further

128

and I can see water at the bottom.'

'He'll have to work from the chair, then—pity,' Harold said. 'I'm lowering you down a chip hammer on a free line. Work from the top and mind you don't catch the falling bricks in your lap!'

Harold tied the hammer to a thin line and lowered it gently over the rim of the shaft. 'Here it comes!'

Susan was surprised at how much rope went into a hundred and twenty-five feet but a little later Edward called, 'Got it. What sort of a bloody knot is this?'

The chipping sounded like blows from a sledge hammer and a few moments later they heard the first brick plunge into the water below, ricocheting from the walls as it fell. It was quickly followed by others.

'Careful!' From Harold. 'Don't go mad down there!'

In less than five minutes Edward had demolished the grid of bricks. 'I'm through. I'm going in.'

Henry intervened. 'Tell him to wait by the shaft, he's not to go in alone.'

'I'll go down if you like,' Harold volunteered.

'No, you're needed here, I'll go.'

No argument. Harold pointed to a small mound of water-proof clothing. 'I brought some gear along in case we needed it but there's only the one helmet. See if anything in that lot fits you.' Then he passed the word down to Edward.

The chair was hauled up and Henry seated himself in it though it was a longer and more hazardous business than with Edward, for Henry was neither so practised nor so agile. He carried a stick and he had a powerful hand torch in his belt. Susan noticed that the mood of the party had changed. Now that there seemed to be a real prospect of getting into the mine everyone was sobered. In half an hour or less they would probably know.

At first Henry found it difficult to correct the tendency to spin but by using the stick in conjunction with his feet, he managed it. The shaft was no more than four feet across. Even the smooth brick walls had collected small pockets of soil which held over-wintering ferns in addition to the algae and lichens which were everywhere. The descent seemed to take a long time but though he had no head for height he was not giddy, probably because the walls were so close. The circle of light at the mouth grew smaller and he could scarcely resist the conclusion that the shaft must taper. The air was fresh and cold with a rich earthy smell, not unpleasant.

'Here you are.' Edward caught the chair and pulled it sideways, partly into the tunnel. 'Don't grab the brickwork! You'll have the bloody lot down on us.'

It was a sprawling, undignified business getting out of the chair.

'Have you brought your own torch?'

Henry switched on his hand torch and swept the beam over the way ahead but a sharp bend only a few yards away prevented him from seeing much. The passage had been cut through solid rock and although Edward had said that it was dry, the walls were covered with a viscous slime and underfoot the rock was made dangerously slippery by a film of mud. Both men were crouched and Henry was subdued by his first experience underground.

'There isn't much room.'

Edward growled, 'What did you expect? Save your moans until you have to breathe in and slide on your belly, head down.' He stood nonchalantly on the edge of the shaft and spoke to the surface, then he squeezed past Henry . . . 'Here, you wear the helmet and I'll take your torch. I'll go first, I know the ropes.' He seemed to move at an incredible speed and his head never once cracked against the fluctuating ceiling. Henry followed as best he could, often going, unashamedly, on all fours.

If anything the passage got smaller for a time; then, abruptly, it opened out into a small chamber where it was possible to stand upright. Henry stretched luxuriously but Edward hurried him on, 'We don't want to hang about here, this rock is friable.' Certainly, for the first time, the floor was made up of large jagged fragments, presumably dropped from the roof.

After what seemed an interminable time, Edward said,

130

'We've come about a hundred and seventy yards, have you any idea how far it's likely to be?'

It required a major effort for Henry to detach himself from the overwhelming impact of his surroundings and to see what he was doing in perspective. Already he had lost all sense of time and distance. He tried to reason it out. 'The island must be about four hundred yards from the north shore and Roger Leigh's account would make the entrance to the first room about eighty yards in—say another hundred and twenty yards.'

Almost as he finished speaking they came out of a tunnel into a chamber whose dimensions he could only guess at. They seemed to be on a ledge two or three feet wide which ran along one side of it at a height of fifteen to twenty feet.

'Watch your step—it's slippery and you could easily end up down there with a broken neck.'

Henry resolutely kept his torch beam and his eyes on Edward, refusing to look down and in due course they appeared to have traversed the ledge and arrived at another tunnel. Another indeterminate period of creeping along, doubled up, a gait to which he was becoming accustomed, then Edward stopped.

'There's a door.' He moved aside enough to allow Henry to see a heavy wooden door, just the size of the tunnel—about three and a half feet square.

The door was already a little ajar and it opened the rest of the way without difficulty and they were in the second cavern but this one was much smaller—no larger than an ordinary room and they had entered it at floor level.

'It's a room!' Edward exclaimed.

It was true, the walls were of cut stone and the floor of rectangular slabs. With his torch, Henry picked out the wooden bench, the rack against the wall, even the hook in the ceiling, but there were no instruments of torture, no whips, and above all no body. Henry breathed a sigh of relief.

'This was one of Joseph's secret rooms,' Henry said. 'This is what it was all about.'

'Not a very cheery spot,' Edward offered, directing his torch all round the place. 'I could think of better places to

131

bring a girl, but at least it's dry.' After the damp slime of the workings the air felt dry and fresh.

'Perhaps the next room will be more to your liking—I hope so.'

For once Henry could not analyse his own feelings, blended as they were of satisfaction, hope and fear, veined through with excitement, for beyond that door—and there was a door —there might be not only the girl they were seeking, living or dead, but a collection of Chinese *objets d'art* which even if it consisted wholly of contemporary pieces would have great interest and considerable value.

'After you.' Edward had done his piece.

Henry lifted the latch and tried to convince himself that all he wanted to see was little Wong Mei Mei alive and well. It *was* all he wanted, the place could be a bare cavern like the first if she were alive.

'Now all we can do is wait.' Harold moved away from the shaft, perched himself on one of the stay rods of the winch and started to fill his pipe. His men gathered in a group and chatted in low tones. The policeman paced slowly up and down as though patrolling his beat. Johnny still stared at the mouth of the shaft as though transfixed and Susan sensed that he had suffered an overwhelming disappointment. The mist still lingered, the island seemed cut off, it was a strange experience—depressing—the excitement had departed. She shivered and drew her coat about her.

Johnny turned away from the shaft at last, caught sight of her, but his gaze swept over her, indifferent; then, suddenly, he brightened and his smile came back. He came over, took her hand and tried to lead her toward the path out of the clearing. Harold saw him and intervened but Susan felt sorry for his dumb animal suffering. 'It's all right, Mr. Vane, Johnny and I get on well.' She hoped that it was true but she felt less happy when Johnny led her to the punt and wanted her to get in, but she did. She tried to tell him that she could not punt but he took no notice, instead he loosed the painter, picked up the pole, fended off expertly and brought the little craft round the island. He pointed to the shore where, presumably, the Pavilion was, but it was still not possible to see across the lake. He seemed to know it well for he never lost bottom once and in a surprisingly short space of time they were alongside the floating jetty under the willow tree. In a flash Johnny was out of the punt making it fast, then he beckoned her with every appearance of urgency. He led her along inside the ornamental stone railing to a point where it passed within two or three feet of the wall of the Pavilion. The carved balustrade had been erected on a stone plinth and the ground inside the barrier, between it and the Pavilion, was tiled with small hexagonal tiles each about six inches across.

Johnny stopped and knelt down on the wet tiles, then with the blade of a clasp knife he prised up one of the tiles nearest to the balustrade. The tile came up easily but revealed nothing more than the mortar underneath. Johnny grasped a section of the stone plinth, and without any apparent effort twisted it through a right angle; it rotated smoothly and disclosed a small gap just large enough for him to insert his hand. Susan was standing close, watching, but now he waved her back and was not satisfied until she had retreated four or five feet; then, he gave his wrist a sudden twist and a section of the ground between them subsided—not violently but gently, obviously hinged and carefully counterpoised. Susan hardly knew what she had been expecting but she was astonished by what she saw—not that it was remarkable if you accepted Roger's story, for there was the spiral staircase, and five or six feet down was the landing on which he had fallen, wrenching his ankle, a hundred and forty years ago. Obviously Roger had released the catch mechanism while standing on the door. The door was roughly circular in shape though its perimeter was irregular, being determined by the junction lines between the hexagonal tiles.

So this was Joseph's secret—or the way to it. But what was she to do now? There was no doubt what Johnny intended, he stood watching her with every sign of impatience and anticipation. She might have excused herself, reasonably, from

133

penetrating into what must be pitch darkness below, had it not been for the electric torch which rested on a ledge above the landing. Evidence at least that the place was still being used. She would have to take a look, go part of the way at least, and she felt reassured by the fact that she would have Johnny's fearsome bulk beside her. She hoped that she was right in assuming that he was on the side of the angels. But Johnny had other ideas. When she tried to encourage him to go down the steps he drew back in terror and she was sure that he would have run away altogether if she persisted. He was like a child.

She stepped down to the landing, reached for the torch and turned to look up at his great moon face peering down at her. He was solemn now, frightened. She was frightened too, her heart thumped so violently she thought she was going to faint. What if Johnny closed the trap door? What if . . .? One hundred and fifty steps, Roger had said; she would count them to save her wits. She miscounted and gave up but it seemed a long way. After the first couple of turns in the stair she was in darkness and dependent on her torch. With difficulty she resisted the temptation to go back to see if the trap was still open. At last she reached bottom and her torch beam showed a long narrow passage sloping gently to a door at the end, just as Roger had said. The roof, walls and floor were all of cut stone and the passage was dry with a current of fresh air streaming past her. She reached the door 'with a latch of iron such as are found in churches'. Now was the time to turn back; honour had been satisfied and it would be foolhardy to go on. Mei Mei might be on the other side of that door but it was equally probable that Leigh would be there too. Henry and Edward would reach them, of that she felt confident now, but when? But if minutes counted, and they might . . . She lifted her hand to the latch—'scarce knowing whether I would have it yield or no'—but as for Roger, so for her, the door opened easily and she switched off her torch.

There was the room. It took her a moment to realize that it was lit, for the lighting was dim and seemed to come from a single source somewhere at the far end and low down. But it was enough to show her the main features of the room, to catch the glowing colours. She was aware of furniture, screens and draperies, but form merged into shadow and was lost. She recognized the thin lingering fragrance of incense. She must be underneath the lake but there was no trace of mustiness.

'Is anybody there?' Her voice sounded cracked and unfamiliar.

Utter silence. In fact she realized that it was the silence which oppressed her most, it seemed unnatural. Like Roger, she advanced slowly down the middle of the room, an aisle between vaguely perceived tables, cabinets, chests, disposed more as they would be in a museum. She reached a lacquered screen at the far end and she felt sure that it must be the screen Roger had described which hid the divan, and it was from the other side of the screen that the light came. She would have liked to call out but she could not bear the prospect of hearing her own voice again cutting through the silence. She stood listening but only to hear the sound of her heart, then she crept round the screen. What she saw was by no means frightening. In soft light, lamp light, two figures lying on the divan as though asleep, both in embroidered silk robes. One was Francis Leigh, the other Mei Mei, that much she could see though their faces were in shadow. Now she spoke; what she said, she hardly knew, but it made no difference for there was no response from the figures on the divan. Leigh was nearest to her and she went to him, shining her torch on his face. He was lying on his back, his eyes wide and staring up into the shadows. Clotted blood caked his lips and nostrils. His right arm hung limp, trailing the carpet, and near the fingers was a small pearl-handled revolver.

Susan was no longer frightened, only shocked. If Leigh had killed himself there was little hope for Mei Mei. She hurried round the bed and bent over the girl. The silk robe was open and she was naked underneath, her skin was cold to the touch and Susan shuddered, but there was no sign of any wound.

At that moment she heard Henry's voice, quite close, on

the other side of the screen; just three words: 'This is it!'

Seconds of confusion, of explanation, of reproof, then they were by the bed, their torch beams lighting the scene weirdly. Henry was bending over Mei Mei. 'She's alive! But she won't be much longer unless we get her out of here.'

'Is she injured?'

'I don't think so, she's been drugged.'

They wrapped her in their coats. Edward stood looking down at his brother as though he could not credit what he saw. Henry spoke sharply, 'For Christ's sake, Leigh, snap out of it! Get out there and tell that policeman to radio for a doctor, ambulance, stretcher—the lot.'

'Not that way!'

Edward had turned back the way he and Henry had come. She watched him moving like a sleepwalker and prayed that Johnny had not closed the trap door.

But it was very odd. Suddenly this secret and eerie place had lost its power over her. Now it was just a rather foolishly elaborate stage set which had become the scene of tragedy; only the two figures on the bed belonged to the real world and they were all that mattered.

CHAPTER ELEVEN

INTERROGATION—BLESSED WORD, dear to the hearts of policemen everywhere. Even though what happened now seemed clear enough, even though Superintendent Judd was satisfied that he had the culprit safely tucked away in a re-frigerated drawer at the mortuary, questions must be asked and answered, the answers written down and turned into long statements full of gobbledygook.

'When did you last see Sir Francis?' and, with a certain ferocious good humour, 'Where were you, say, between ten and midnight last night?'

A few of the answers were relevant.

Flossie said: 'Sir Francis usually goes to his room after the evening meal and I go along to see if he wants anything round about half past eight. After that I reckon I've finished for the night.'

'You did so last night?'

'Yes.' She hesitated as though about to say something surprising, 'Mr. Gerald was there with him.' Flossie's eyes were red rimmed in grotesque contrast with her natural pallor. She was resentful, apprehensive, unsure whether she was being invited to weight the scales yet more heavily against Sir Francis or whether there was a grain of hope to be derived from the continuing enquiry.

'You seem to have been surprised to find Mr. North in Sir Francis's room. Was it so unusual?'

Flossie twisted an old-fashioned cameo-ring on her bony finger. 'I've never known it happen before in the years since Mr. Gerald came.'

'Didn't they get on?'

She made an irritable movement to express her frustration through lack of words. 'You could say that. They were two men as different as chalk from cheese. They just didn't have anything in common.'

Judd looked at her over his spectacles. 'Except Mrs. North, the house, the estate and most of the details of their home life.'

Flossie pursed her lips. 'It might seem like that to a stranger but actually Mr. Gerald was nothing more than a sort of lodger. I've never liked the man but you can't help feeling sometimes . . .' She broke off. 'At any rate they never saw much of each other except at meal times.'

'Last night when you found them together in Sir Francis's room—had they been quarrelling, do you think?'

She was decisive. 'Nothing like that. They weren't the sort to quarrel.'

'But you had the impression that something was wrong?'

'No, not wrong—they were concerned about something and they didn't want to be bothered with me.' She said it with the resignation of one who has had to discipline herself to

137

the whims of others.

'Was that the last time you saw Sir Francis?'

'Yes.'

'What about Mr. North?'

'What about him?'

'Did you see him again before you went to bed?'

'No, I didn't.' She hesitated and looked suddenly cunning. 'But I did hear someone come in around midnight.'

'Surely that would have been Mrs. North—wasn't she at a dance?'

Flossie nodded. 'She was, she went to the dance run by her *League of Helpers*, but it wasn't Miss Lucy I heard, it was a man.'

'How do you know?'

'Footsteps.'

'Mr. North?'

She shrugged. 'The attic where I sleep is over his room and I heard somebody moving about down there.'

'How many telephones are there in this house?' The question came from Henry who had not spoken so far.

She considered. 'Four. One in Miss Lucy's flat, one in Sir Francis's room, one in the library and then there's one in the hall where the switch box is—just outside this door.'

'Do you operate the switch box?'

'Sometimes. Mostly I've got something better to do.' Her manner toward Henry was especially curt, she seemed to feel that in some way he had let her down.

'And then all the instruments are left through to the exchange?'

'Sir Francis's and Miss Lucy's are.'

'And that was the case last night?'

'It always is in the evenings.'

'Did the telephone ring at all after dinner?'

'It rang just before I went up to bed but somebody must have answered it pretty quick because it only gave a couple of rings.'

'Would you have heard if someone made a call from the instrument in the hall outside?'

'I'm not deaf.'

'Did anyone make a call?'

'Not while I was in the kitchen here they didn't.'

Henry seemed to have run out of questions and Judd took over. 'Did you hear a car driving off either before or just after you went to bed?'

'I believe I heard a car sometime during the evening but I can't remember when it was.'

'Think!'

She bridled. 'I am thinking but what's the good. There's one or other in and out all the time and I don't take that much notice.'

Judd's men had found Sir Francis's car abandoned. It had been driven in among the trees of the *Pinetum* just off the estate road which led to the Vanes'.

Gerald North did not put down his pen when they came in. His attitude was that of a man facing an unwelcome interruption and anxious to keep it as short as possible. On the table in front of him, open, was the folder containing photographs of various treasures of Chinese art which Henry had seen when he visited the room alone. Gerald had been making notes in his fine spidery writing in the broad margins of the photographs.

Judd was polite but official. Henry recognized the policeman's inbred wariness of lawyers. 'You understand, sir, that I have to enquire into the events leading to Sir Francis's death and the assault on Miss Wong.'

A vague gesture, possibly assent. North nodded toward the telephone, 'I rang the hospital a few minutes ago, they tell me that her condition is critical.'

'So I believe, sir.'

'A terrible business, Superintendent.'

'Yes. Now, sir, one or two questions and I shan't keep you long. You have already said that you telephoned the hospital last night asking for Miss Wong to be released from duty. I would like you to tell me in detail of the events which led up to your making that call.'

'Francis came to my room and told me that . . .'

'What time was this, sir?'

'A few minutes before ten.'

'Then will you begin earlier, say at eight-thirty when you were with Sir Francis in his room.'

A thin, slightly contemptuous smile. 'You've been talking to the housekeeper.'

'It's my job to talk to anybody with information to give, sir. You must know that.'

'I do, Superintendent. I do.'

'Then perhaps you will tell me how you came to be with Sir Francis and the subject of your conversation with him?'

North had dropped any pretence of waiting for them to go. 'You are quite right, of course.' He took a tablet from a box on the table, removed the wrapping and slipped the tablet into his mouth. Then he sat back in his chair, fixed his gaze on a framed specimen of calligraphy which hung over the fire place and seemed to address himself to it. 'Yesterday evening as I was passing his room the door was open and he called me in. This in itself was unusual; I don't suppose that I have been in that room more than three times since coming to *Peel*.' He paused without removing his gaze from the calligraphy. Judd and Henry remained silent.

'Francis was agitated and it was obvious that he wanted to confide in me but that he had difficulty in putting what he wanted to say into words. At last, without preamble, it came, "Gerald," he said. "I want you to tell me if you think I am mad."' For the first time North's stare dropped from the frame to his desk and he began to fiddle with an ebony ruler. 'I tried to turn the question off in a lighthearted way by saying that it depended on one's definitions of sanity and madness but this only made him irritable. "I want a straight answer," he said. "Am I the sort of madman who would be better locked up?"' The lawyer raised his eyes momentarily and met Judd's. 'It was a terrible moment for me—and for him. When it comes to the point you cannot tell a man that he is mad. I said that the mere asking of such a question seemed to mean that he needed professional advice and that he should consult
140

a first class alienist. To my surprise, the suggestion pleased him; he said that I was a good friend and that he would think it over.'

'And then?'

North looked up sharply, as though recalled from far away. 'Then I left him and went to my own part of the house. Between nine-thirty and ten I decided to have a bath and while I was still in the bathroom I heard the telephone ring in this room. It rang only twice and I assumed that someone must have answered it. A few minutes later Francis arrived. I was afraid that he had come to pick up our conversation where it had been left but he now seemed much more relaxed and made no reference to it. He told me of the cable for Mei Mei and asked me to ring the hospital. I did so and offered to go to meet the girl but he pointed out that Lucy was using our car and said that he would go himself.'

North took a deep breath and looking at Judd, he said, 'At that time, Francis's behaviour was perfectly normal, and though it may sound incredible to you, it did not occur to me to question either the truth of his tale or the wisdom of allowing him to go to meet Mei Mei.' It was almost as though he was making a formal statement. 'Of course, I shall find it difficult to forget that.'

Judd was sympathetic. 'I shouldn't take it too much to heart, sir. It is one thing to theorize but quite another to *act* in a manner which assumes the guilt of someone close to you.'

The lawyer nodded. 'I have discovered the truth of that.'

Henry spoke for the first time. 'And then you went out?'

North looked at him quickly. 'Did I?'

'The housekeeper says that she heard you come in around midnight,' Judd said.

Henry saw the flicker of surprise on the lawyer's face. 'Did she? I had no idea I made so much noise.'

'But you were out?'

'Yes, I was out, Dr. Pym.'

'Doing what, sir?' From Judd.

'Walking, just walking, Superintendent.'

'Around the estate?'

North nodded. 'I often take a walk before bedtime, I find that it prepares me for sleep, but I admit that last night I stayed out much longer than usual. I wanted to think.' He straightened the blotter on his desk. 'I tried to decide what, if anything, I ought to do.'

'And you reached a conclusion?'

'I decided to be quite open with Dr. Pym, to take him fully into my confidence and to be guided by his advice. Of course, I was too late.'

Judd preened his moustache between finger and thumb. 'You went out shortly after Sir Francis?'

'Shortly after, yes.'

'Did you see him return from the hospital?'

'I saw the lights of his car as he drove along the estate road toward the Vanes'.'

'But you did not see him come back to this house?'

'How could I? It seems that he did not return.'

Judd nodded. 'Precisely. If you were out until midnight didn't it strike you as odd that Sir Francis had not come back to the house by that time?'

'Frankly I never thought about it but if I had I doubt if it would have occurred to me as important. If he had gone to the Vanes' as I assumed that he had, it would have been natural for Harold to invite him in for a drink.'

Judd glanced at Henry and Henry shook his head. Judd stood up, 'Very well, sir, thank you for your help.'

North continued to stare down at his desk and said nothing.

Henry was not present when they interviewed Harold Vane but he saw the transcript:

'Last evening I worked in the office until after eight when I watched television for a while. I went to bed at about half-past ten.'

'Did you telephone *Peel* during the evening?'

'No.'

'Did you have any contact with Sir Francis?'

'Not after five o'clock when I called at the house to talk over some estate business.'

'Did Sir Francis seem normal at that time?'

'Perfectly. Worried but normal.'

'You were alone in the house last night, Mr. Vane?'

'Yes, my wife and daughter were staying with friends in Penzance.'

'Is it true that two or three years back you contemplated writing a history of the estate?'

'I still do but so far I've done nothing about it.'

'Did Sir Francis authorize you to use the contents of the chest which contained the letters and diaries of Joseph and Roger Leigh?'

'He did but I never got round to it.'

When Lucy North was questioned Henry was there. She said that she had been to a Christmas Dance organized by her *League of Helpers*. 'I used Gerald's car and when I got back it was nearly three.'

'Did you see anyone about the estate?'

A momentary hesitation. 'At three in the morning?'

'Did your husband wait up for you?'

'No.'

'So that you saw no one before going to bed either around the estate or in the house?'

'No one.'

'You are quite sure?' From Henry.

A faint flush of colour in her cheeks. 'I am quite sure, Dr. Pym.'

'She is lying,' Henry said to Judd afterwards.

Anticlimax, the emotional reaction to tension, a dulling of perception and a feeling of futility. Henry was off on some project of his own, the estate was alive with policemen in and out of uniform, the press was infiltrating and the family seemed to have melted away. Susan was left on her own and she decided to go for a walk. Inevitably, it seemed, she found herself on the way to Edward's cottage. She was surprised by the activity along the estate road, two police cars passed her, an open sports car containing two tweedy types wedged in

143

by photographic gear, a Land Rover and a policeman on a bike.

Edward was subdued; not surprising. It takes more than an average ration of imperturbability to find your brother's body and to accept that he has shot himself after a couple of kinky sex murders. Even though—perhaps especially when —you half believe that this sort of thing runs in the family.

A truck loaded with assorted ironmongery rattled along the road. 'Busy!' Susan said inanely.

'More like London every day,' Edward agreed. He took her coat. 'Come upstairs out of this bloody mausoleum.'

He sat on the floor by the window and after a moment's hesitation she sat by him. The window was so low that they could still see out.

A police car swished by.

'They seem to have enough police on the job.' Susan tried to make conversation.

'I've had two of them here.'

'What doing?'

'Asking questions. Routine they said.'

A grey afternoon, a thin steady drizzle swept every now and then by a gusting wind. Not far away a motor spluttered into life, coughed a couple of times then settled down to a steady throbbing roar.

'What are they doing?'

'Taking the place apart, I should think. They've brought in a team of miners from Camborne. I suppose they're searching for the bodies.' He broke off, 'Any more news of Mei Mei?'

'She's still unconscious and they say that her condition is critical.'

She knew that he wanted to talk, that he wanted her to talk but she could think of nothing to say that was neither banal nor offensive. How do you show sympathy to a man without laying yourself wide open? Henry sometimes accused her of being hard but it wasn't true, it was just that she had never learned the knack of showing sympathy. Why the hell couldn't she make the right responses? It worried her. Millions of pudding-headed women got and kept their men with

144

nothing else to offer. But it was no help.

'I see the press have moved in.'

He nodded. 'It's a field day for the bastards. Think of the headlines! *The Lake Murders, Death in the Willow Garden, The Monster in the Mine* . . . They can't lose.' He traced a match-stick figure in the condensation on the window pane. 'You knew Frankie, Susan, did he strike you as a monster? Somehow you expect it to show. Not that I knew him all that well although he was my brother, he was twenty-one when I was born. Even so . . .'

He sat back resting his weight on his hands, staring up at the ceiling. 'I thought it might have been his idea to suggest a link between the disappearances and the Joseph legend. He had a twisted sense of humour and he would have been quite capable of setting the police off on a wild goose chase of which he had a grandstand view. In his younger days he had a reputation as a rather tedious practical joker but I never thought of him as violent.'

He turned to face her as though he wanted to measure the effect of his words. 'Francis may have been the sort of man who liked to shed his inhibitions with his shirt but he wasn't a sadist—at least, I don't think so.'

Susan was trying hard to forestall silence. 'Some practical jokes border on the sadistic but I agree, I wouldn't have thought him capable of physical cruelty. But if he did kidnap and murder the girls, why did he invite Henry here? Surely he must have realized the risk he ran? Even if it was Gerald's idea, he didn't have to agree to it.'

Edward shook his head. 'That I could understand. He was an exhibitionist, never averse to an audience. Even his periodic jags had their public relations angle. A man in his position could have gone up to town and had all the women he wanted without a breath of scandal, instead he chose to advertise his indiscretions by performing in his own backyard.' He paused thoughtfully. 'In many ways Frankie was immature, like a smutty-minded schoolboy who gets a kick out of writing on lavatory walls—and putting his name at the bottom.' He picked at a blob of crimson paint stuck to a floorboard. 'Another thing that puzzles me is the business of the clothes I found. Why should he pinch your boss's car to dump them? Unless it was sheer bravado . . .'

'You don't think that he deliberately set out to involve someone else?'

Edward stopped short. 'Is that what your boss thinks?'

'He doesn't often confide in me.'

It was evidently a new idea to Edward and he was impressed. 'You could be right. It was that business which latched the thing firmly on to *Peel*. It may be that he intended it to go further and to point the finger at one of us—at Gerald, or me, or even Harold.'

Susan was stiff through sitting on the floor and she got up, flexing her limbs. She walked over to one of the picture stacks and started to turn them over. After a moment he came and stood beside her, offering staccato remarks on the pictures, prodding her to criticism. He seemed dissatisfied until he had extracted some wry comment, undiluted approval would not do. Perhaps after all he was a different kind of man, one who set little value on tea and sympathy. Perhaps he liked a woman to keep her claws out.

They were very close and quite suddenly she was overwhelmed by a longing for him. Perhaps some tiny unconscious movement, some subtle change in her attitude communicated itself, for in a moment he had his arms round her. His hands explored expertly under her clothing, his fingers hard and sure, kneaded her flesh. He must have known that she was his for the taking but instead he drew away.

'Aren't you afraid of me?'

'No.' It was true, she wasn't afraid, only angry.

'I am.'

'Afraid of yourself?'

'Of heredity.' He walked away, back to the window and stood looking out.

She spoke with more heat than she intended. 'That is just damned nonsense.'

'I know what you are going to say. You can't inherit a habit of kidnapping and murdering girls—right?'

146

'Dead right!'

'But you can inherit a tendency toward certain abnormal patterns of behaviour—right?'

'More or less, I suppose, but you Leighs are obsessed by your heredity. Few enough families can trace their ancestry beyond great-grandparents. If I have a Joseph in my family tree, I'm blissfully unaware of the fact.'

'Bully for you! But you haven't, as far as I know, had a sister who died in a lunatic asylum, a nephew like Johnny nor a brother who turned out to be a sex murderer.'

She was chastened. 'I'm sorry, but you can't live with ghosts. You have to believe that you know yourself and have faith in your own individuality, in the integrity of your own personality. It's all you've got, all any of us have.'

He turned from the window to face her. 'Have you got that faith?'

'In myself?'

'In me.'

She smiled. 'Other things being equal I'd take a chance.'

He looked at her, startled, then he came over and put his hands on her shoulders. 'What the hell does that mean? No, don't tell me.' He continued to hold her and to look into her eyes but she could make nothing of his expression.

'Do you like custard?'

'Not particularly.'

'Sliced bread?'

'It's a capitalist plot against the masses.'

He nodded. 'There! I knew that we were soul mates.'

You could never tell with Edward.

'Let's go and see what those bastards are doing in the mine.'

She was obedient. He helped her on with her coat and they went out into the dusk. Still misty rain, the air tainted with the acrid fumes of diesel exhaust. They could hear the motor throbbing away and over to their left a lurid glow flared above the trees.

They walked down through the wood, a short cut to the lake, and came out on the grassy slopes above it. Upwards of half a dozen vehicles were parked there and one, an open truck, carried a generator now almost deafeningly obtrusive. Groups of men stood about gossiping and smoking. Cables snaked across the grass and down into the lake. Out on the island a hidden flood lamp produced an eerie effect through the mist like a submarine volcano in eruption. On the other side of the lake the Pavilion loomed against a background of diffused though powerful light.

'I hope you realize you had a narrow escape just now.'

'You oversell your virility like a detergent. It only makes the customer wonder whether there is anything in the packet after all.'

He took her arm and squeezed it. 'Bitch!'

They crossed the timber bridge, passed under the willow and round the Pavilion. A white lamp slung high was winning hands down against the fading daylight. Two constables fended off half a dozen press men.

'Dr. Pym's secretary.'

'Mr. Edward Leigh.'

It worked. Down the steps, no need for a torch now, a string of lights hung from the stone walls like a fairground. But the room itself was their biggest surprise. Brilliantly lit, alive with men, not an ounce of mystery left, not an atom of fear. A saleroom being got ready for public viewing, a storeroom in a museum. Susan was astonished by the dust which lay thick over everything and by the way the colours were bleached by the white light. She was glad that the room had suffered this indignity for all the misery, suffering and fear it had witnessed.

Henry was standing by a lacquered cabinet which, on its legs, stood half his height. He looked pale and tired but he smiled when he saw her. Edward wandered off and left them together.

Gerald North was there, moving round like a man in a trance. He seemed to be examining everything minutely and from time to time he would put out his hand to touch a piece of furniture, a porcelain vase or a jade ornament, but though Susan watched him closely she never once saw his fingers make

148

contact, it was as though he were afraid that the things would vanish at his touch.

'Well, Mr. North, what do you think of it as a collection?'

North was startled by Henry's voice. He faced round, blinking, as though he had been brought suddenly from darkness into a bright light. Then he recovered himself and Susan was intrigued to see his features assume their accustomed mould, expressing an ingrained caution, betraying that deep vein of cynicism which was the product of his nature and of his profession.

He came over to them, suave, pedantic. 'It's difficult to say. This is not, of course, a collection in any technical sense— merely an assemblage.' He made a small gesture at the random scene. 'But one could hardly expect a museum of Chinese art. In Joseph's day, despite the vogue for Chinoiserie, the western world knew almost nothing of the art of China at first hand. Only a trickle of stuff found its way through to the west and it came chiefly through Holland.'

'Mostly contemporary porcelain, I suppose,' Henry said.

Gerald nodded. ''And there's plenty of that here, some of it is interesting and quite valuable. There also seems to be some original lacquered furniture, the small cabinets are probably genuinely Chinese, imported before Joseph's time, the larger items are almost certainly Dutch or English but none the less valuable on that account, some English craftsmen produced imitations of the Chinese model which were superior to the native work.' He nodded several times as though in confirmation of unexpressed thoughts. 'The jade looks good but there's very little of it, and as for the metalwork . . .' He gave a short dry laugh. 'Much of that must have come from bazaars all over the orient.' He walked over to an ornate lantern-like object, seemed about to pick it up, then changed his mind. 'Perhaps some of it was made in Birmingham.'

Henry smiled politely. 'What about the carpets and tapestries—could they be Turkish?'

Gerald gave him a sharp look. 'Possibly. I have no knowledge of Turkish art but I can say that they are certainly not Chinese.' His manner had changed abruptly; he glanced at his

149

watch. 'I am afraid I must return to the house, perhaps you will excuse me.'

'And so saying he swep' out!' Susan said.

They found Judd in a cleared area, seated at a table with a telephone, for all the world like the clerk of the sale. He looked up from a sheaf of papers with tired eyes. 'This must be the weirdest Murder H.Q. yet.'

'Anything new?'

Judd shook his head. 'Precious little.' He nodded toward the far end of the chamber, 'You know what it's like beyond there. The miners have found half a dozen small shafts going down to adit level and they are investigating all of them. So far they've found a few bones.'

'Human?'

'Slade, the pathologist, has had a look at them and he says they belonged to three young adult females but they've been there a hell of a long time.'

'Joseph's work.'

'It seems so.' Matter of fact, prosaic. Ancient tragedy must be turned into literature if it is to tug at the heart strings.

'No signs of the missing girls?'

The superintendent pointed to two piles of clothes placed on a mat on the floor and two handbags, one with a shoulder strap. 'That's all we've found so far—Leigh's clothes and the little Chinese girl's. The shoulder bag belongs to her too but the other we can't account for. I sent it to the girls' mothers but they can't identify it. Perhaps you would take a look at it, Susan?'

Susan picked up the unidentified bag. Imitation snake skin, the sort of bag you could buy in any chain store for a quid. She opened it and sniffed inside. Nothing exclusive in the way of cosmetics either. She tipped the contents on to the table. A compact, lipstick, a packet of *Player's Gold Leaf* with four cigarettes left in it, a cheap lighter, a ball point pen, a purse containing twelve shillings and ninepence and a sachet of *Aspro*. The bag could have belonged to any working girl who had to make a little go a long way. But there was one thing more, two stamps each with a bit of stamp edging attached. Susan pointed to them. 'These date it more or less. They're the higher values of a commemorative issue put on sale on the fifteenth or sixteenth of this month.'

'Good for you!' Judd said.

'I collect stamps.' Modestly. 'She probably does too, or perhaps she bought them for a brother or sister.'

Judd was grave, answering his own thoughts. 'These days it's possible for a girl to be missing a fortnight without anybody even noticing, especially if she lives alone.' The disintegration of family life was one of the Superintendent's chief quarrels with the modern world.

'Odd that there should be only a handbag,' Henry said. He perched himself on the edge of an elaborately carved chest. 'What did Slade have to say about Leigh?'

'Officially there's been no report yet, privately he assures me that Leigh died of a bullet wound in a manner consistent with suicide.'

'And Mei Mei? Any further news from the hospital?'

'I've had word to say that she has recovered consciousness and seems to be over the worst. No questions yet, though.'

'Good for Mei Mei! You've got someone with her?'

Judd looked at him sharply. 'A W.P.C. in her room.'

'Day and night?'

'Yes, but it's only a formality, she can't tell us much that we don't already know.'

'That remains to be seen.'

Judd took out his pipe and began to fill it. 'Get it off your chest, Henry.'

'These pressmen, will they get an account of all this into their evening editions?'

Judd grinned. 'They'll be out of a job if they don't.'

'How much did you tell them? Did you mention the missing girls?'

Judd put a match to his pipe. 'I didn't have to, they were well briefed before they got to me.'

'So that the girls' names will be in this evening's papers?'

The Superintendent looked puzzled. 'I imagine so—why?'

'And on the radio and television news bulletins?'

'That's less certain, they are more cagey about naming names.'

Henry looked at his watch. 'Then ring them up. It's a quarter to seven now, you could make sure that the names are used in their main bulletins.'

Judd hesitated. 'I hope I know what you're thinking. Anyway, it can't do any harm.' He picked up the telephone.

Henry looked at the instrument dubiously. 'Does that thing work?'

'Of course.'

Henry shook his head. 'The Administrative Machine will turn a tomb into an office as promptly as fairy godmothers turn pumpkins into coaches! I'll bet they did the same at Auschwitz.'

Judd grimaced comically at Susan. 'Do you know what he's talking about?'

Henry was restless. He prowled with Susan at his heels. In one screened-off area they found two cylinders of bottled gas, a hotplate and a couple of gas heaters. A cupboard contained a stock of tinned food and a quantity of utensils. There was a chemical closet but no water supply that they could find.

'It must have been quite a job, equipping this place and keeping it supplied in secret,' Susan said.

'The man had a vision and visions drive men to desperate lengths.'

'You sound almost sorry for him.'

'No, I'm not sorry for him though perhaps I ought to be.'

When they returned Judd had finished telephoning. 'Have you been over this place for prints?' Henry enquired.

The Superintendent looked at him as though he had taken leave of his senses. 'Don't be absurd, Henry, it would take a year.'

But Henry was impatient. 'Not everything, just the articles which have been in regular use—the cooking utensils, the closet, that sort of thing.'

Judd considered. 'It might be worth it.'

152

'I'm sure that it would.'

Judd smoked in silence for a while then he said, 'One question. Have you made up your mind that this is not a murder case after all?'

'On the contrary, I'm quite sure that it is.'

CHAPTER TWELVE

S U S A N S A T O P P O S I T E Henry at the breakfast table; there was no one else, for the Norths breakfasted in their rooms. Henry emptied his second cup of coffee and, as many men by reflex action reach for their cigarettes, so Henry patted his pockets in search of his pill bottle. This month it was yeast. He tipped a couple of small dirty-brown tablets on to the white cloth. 'Try these, Susan, brewer's yeast. Through your obstinate adherence to white bread you may well be suffering from thiamine deficiency.'

'No thank you, I've tried them before, they look like rabbit droppings and they taste like dried blood.'

Luckily Flossie came in with the papers. 'You asked for these.' She was still distant in her manner.

Sir Francis must have had a catholic taste in newspapers —five of them, spanning the whole range of appeal, and in all but one *Peel* had made the front page.

DEATH IN WILLOW PATTERN!

MURDER IN THE WILLOW GARDEN?

THE SECRET CHAMBER OF DEATH!

THE MONSTER IN THE MINE!

The headlines were predictable, so was most of the text but the popular papers gave more space to the missing girls. Two of them reported interviews with the girls' mothers.

Has History Repeated Itself?
Tonight, as we go to press, two women, ordinary house-
wives, Mrs. Valerie Cassels and Mrs. Brenda Ford, are facing
the agonizing possibility that their daughters have fallen
victim to a modern Bluebeard . . .

Henry read conscientiously through all the reports and seemed satisfied. Susan glanced through them with a feeling of revulsion but she had to admit that had she not been involved her reaction would have been quite different. 'I suppose it's quite certain that these girls have been murdered?'

Her question seemed to irritate him and he answered curtly, 'I think that we may soon know.'

She refused to be snubbed. 'It seems to me that apart from the anonymous letters, only two things link the disappearances with *Peel* . . .'

'Oh? And what are they?'

'The cross and the clothes which Edward found.'

Henry shook his head. 'The cross, certainly, but the clothes might have belonged to anybody. I've checked with Judd: a brassière, briefs, a slip, a suspender belt, and a pair of stockings—all from Marks and Spencer's. The sizes are more or less right for either of the girls and for a few hundred thousand others.'

'So it depends on the cross alone.'

'You sound like Billy Graham but you have the right idea.'

Susan sipped cold coffee. 'What did you make of the second handbag—the one I found the stamps in?'

To her surprise, Henry grinned. 'You should have worked that out for yourself.'

Susan tried again. 'If Francis did not kidnap either of the missing girls, where does Mei Mei come into it? Surely she must be part of the same pattern?'

He took this more seriously. 'Crime isn't a chess problem, Susan. There can be no dependence on mathematical logic as a tool for unravelling the workings of the human mind. The greater part of human behaviour is based on rationalization of emotional preference and prejudice and it is because of that that detection remains more of an art than a science.'

'What am I expected to make of that?'

'Very little at the moment but don't look for too much cold logic behind all this.'

They were interrupted again by Flossie but this time she brought the Superintendent with her. Although he could have had little sleep, Judd looked fresh and relaxed. He joined them at the table and accepted Flossie's offer of fresh coffee.

'Mei Mei has made a statement.'

'She's all right?' From Susan.

Judd grinned. 'She's fine. A bit confused but she'll be out and about in a day or two.' Susan's heart warmed to him for his obvious pleasure in the news he gave.

'Concussed?' Henry inquired.

'She collected a bump on the base of her skull. It seems that she was slugged from behind but she has no idea who by.'

Henry resisted the temptation to ask questions and allowed the Superintendent to tell his own story. 'Nobody came to meet her, she walked all the way alone until she came to the point where we found Sir Francis's car and there or thereabouts she was attacked from behind. She remembers nothing much more until she woke in hospital.'

Henry stared at Judd. 'You say "nothing much". Does she remember *anything* that happened in between?'

'Nothing coherent. The doctor says that some things might came back later.'

'What do you make of it?'

Judd toyed with an empty milk jug. 'It doesn't change things much. It's pretty obvious that Leigh arranged with North to meet her but instead he drove to the point where the road to the Vane house passes nearest to the lake and lay in wait for her. He must have carried her down through the trees to the Pavilion—not that there's much of her, poor little soul.'

Flossie came in with fresh coffee. Judd poured himself half a cup of black brew and swallowed it in a single gulp, then patted his moustache with a whiter than white handkerchief. 'What do you think, Henry?'

'I was counting on Mei Mei's statement—when it came —being more informative.'

'I don't see that it matters a great deal. It's not as though the case can ever come to court.'

Later Henry persuaded Judd to walk over the ground. They went out together and Susan went with them. Sunshine; the air moist with the promise of rain; mild, and for a moment it was possible to believe in spring again.

'Wind by nightfall,' Judd said, 'and rain.'

'For God's sake don't go all bucolic,' Henry growled.

Susan had been with Henry on two previous cases working with Judd and she had learned that they always contrived to sound as though they were in the middle of a running fight, with Judd on the defensive. She knew too that it meant nothing.

They followed the main avenue to where the estate road doubled back toward the Vane house and they turned off along it. The surface was pock-marked with pot holes brimming from the recent thaw, rutted with the tracks of heavy farm vehicles, and there were hoof marks in the soft mud. The path was bordered by gloomy thickets of cherry laurel *(Prunus laurocerasus)* and Susan could all too easily imagine Mei Mei, worried, scared, hurrying along, stumbling now and then, her eyes searching the darkness ahead.

They had walked in silence for a long time when Henry said, 'If Leigh intended to kidnap the girl, why didn't he pick her up as arranged and drive along the southern road which passes within yards of the timber bridge? Why waylay her up here and have the job of carrying her over the steepest and roughest ground in the *Pinetum*?'

'I should have thought that was pretty obvious. He didn't want her to know who he was.'

'Rubbish!' Henry stopped to make his point. 'Leigh agreed to fetch Mei Mei from the hospital in his car, thereby making himself accountable for what happened to her. Subsequently his car is found in the *Pinetum* and he is dead in circumstances which point strongly to suicide, with
156

the girl beside him. Does all that suggest that he cared a damn whether his victim recognized him? In any case, on your interpretation of the facts, do you suppose that he intended Mei Mei to survive?'

Judd was placatory. 'I'm not pretending that his actions were logical but can we expect them to have been? According to North he had grave doubts of his own sanity and there is not much in all the events which led up to this to suggest that the mind behind it was normal.'

'You warned me against expecting too much logic,' Susan said.

Henry made an irritable gesture and walked on. Soon they came to the pines. The ground sloped away steeply to their left and the pines clawed at the stony soil with gnarled and twisted roots. 'Would you like to carry a girl down there? Even a little thing like Mei Mei?'

At first Susan did not see the car, then she caught the glint of metal among the trees. It had gone well into the wood probably further than the driver intended.

It was soundless and still under the pines—and cold, for the winter sun could not penetrate the deep chill of the dimly lit aisles. The staid black saloon, its bodywork gleaming, looked absurdly incongruous, its bumper bent round the red fissured trunk of a pine. *(Pinus contorta)* The twisted pine. A constable appeared from nowhere in particular. 'I'm waiting for Marsden's break-down truck, sir. He should be here any minute.'

Henry looked into the car with interest. He tried the driver's door which was locked but the constable had a key. When it was open he told Susan to get in. 'Can you drive like that?' Her feet barely reached the pedals. 'When we borrowed the car from Sir Francis, did you have to adjust the seat?'

Susan shook her head. 'I'm slightly taller than Sir Francis and I was a bit cramped but I didn't bother to alter the seat.'

Susan got out and Henry took her place. His hands rested comfortably on the steering wheel and his feet on the pedals. He looked at Judd.

Judd's face was expressionless. He turned on the constable:
'Were you here when they went over this vehicle?'

'Yes sir.'

'Who did it?' Judd's staccato demands were uncharacteristic and he made the constable nervous.

'Detective Sergeant Moon and Detective Constable Evans, sir.'

'Did they alter the position of the driver's seat?'

The man hesitated. 'No, I don't think so, sir.'

'Are you sure or not?'

'Yes, I'm sure, sir.'

It was then that Susan caught the first glimpse of what must have been in Henry's mind for some time. At first she could hardly credit it, then when she had thought it over it seemed the only possible explanation. The cross was the stumbling block and Henry had said as much at breakfast but she had not understood. Now she did; she understood too why he had crowed over the morning papers. But which of the two men? Then she realized that there were three possibles, not two, and it seemed that Mei Mei had been *carried* down the rough steep path of the *Pinetum*. She shivered.

The rest of the morning passed in dreary frustration for her. They followed Judd's car to Police Headquarters and Henry spent half an hour inside while she waited in the car park. It had started to rain and the town was blanketed in a streaming grey mist. Then she drove Henry and the Superintendent to the Georgian offices of a solicitor. Leigh's solicitor, Henry admitted to her but he would tell her nothing more. Afterwards they returned Judd to his headquarters and lunched in a restaurant by the cathedral where the architecture, the company and the food had a depressingly ecclesiastical flavour. Henry hardly spoke. He was like a tortoise *(Testudo græca)*. You had only to notice that he had his head out for him to pull it in again.

The afternoon was decidedly better. Though with no idea of why or where they were going, Susan drove several miles into the country to a small isolated cottage. Here she was not required to wait in the car but allowed to accompany Henry inside, where they were received very graciously by a tall middle-aged man who stooped, presumably in unconscious adaptation to the low-beamed ceiling and the pygmy-size doors. The cottage was like a museum of Chinese art and Dr. Frere, introduced by Henry as an authority on Chinese bronzes, had what Susan imagined to be the gentle manners and personality of a Confucian sage. He also had a youngish wife, Maria, a Spanish girl, manifestly devoted to him; and numerous Siamese cats. The cats disposed themselves in changing postures of self-conscious elegance among the porcelain, the jade, the ivory and the bronze, and kept Susan's heart in a flutter.

Maria engaged Susan in lively conversation while the two men talked, and though she tried to catch the drift of their discussion, the torrent of Maria's courageous and flamboyant English largely defeated her. They seemed to be discussing a bronze mirror of the T'ang. She caught the evocative words: *The Shield of the Persian Hero, Hamzeh* and something about the Çinili Köşk Museum, Istanbul. Then Maria noticed that the rain had stopped and a watery sunshine encouraged her to show off the garden. Susan spent an enchanting half hour wandering round a maze of mostly stone paths between dripping lush green growth, coming unexpectedly on little arbours with graceful statues of Buddhas or Bodhisattvas, bronze cranes or a temple lantern. She watched the carp in a green translucent pool and in a summer house admired Maria's achievements in the art of *Bonsai*, her gnarled and twisted pines less than eighteen inches high and a Lilliputian oak like a Sherwood giant seen through the wrong end of a telescope. When it rained again and they went back into the cottage, Henry and Dr. Frere were examining a photograph with great attention.

'This was taken when the mirror was loaned by the Turkish authorities to the International Exhibition of Chinese Art in London in 1936. As you see, unlike your specimen, it has two concentric circles of running animals and birds around the central boss—not one.'

'And the diameters differ,' Henry said.

Frere nodded. 'They do, this is given at sixty-eight centimetres while yours, I think, was sixty-nine point five. Both, of course, are very large as these T'ang mirrors go and their size probably accounts for the Turks calling theirs a shield. They captured it in some early sixteenth-century battle and they would have had very little idea what it was.' Frere took his photograph and studied it briefly. 'Take this if you want, and if you ever come across the original of yours I shall be greatly obliged by a sight of it. Believe me, it will cause a stir.'

They drank fragrant tea from porcelain bowls and were at last seen off by Dr. Frere and Maria, standing in the rain, waving until their car disappeared round a bend.

'Have you known the Freres long?'

'I met him first at Oxford.'

Susan wondered how far Henry's way of life had been influenced by this man but Henry's temperament was too volatile for the retired contemplative life to be more than a harmless and interesting pose.

They arrived back at *Peel* as the grey afternoon light retreated before the darkness. The house looked gloomy and deserted and Susan felt weighed down by a massive formless depression. She would have given a great deal never to have to enter that house again. Henry with his disconcerting ability to read her thoughts, put his hand on her arm and said, 'Never mind! We leave tomorrow.'

They put the car away and as they walked back to the house Henry said, 'Judd had an autopsy report on Francis Leigh this morning.' It was as though he were trying to bridge the gap which had grown between them during the day.

Susan was cool. 'Well?'

'He died from the bullet wound but he had taken a considerable though non-fatal quantity of one of the barbiturates.'

'I see.'

Henry looked at her with a wry smile, 'I wonder!' As they were entering the house he added, 'Mei Mei was not sexually assaulted, she is still *virgo intacta.*'

Susan felt relief not entirely on Mei Mei's behalf. 'Good for her!'

'Are you surprised?'

Susan knew this game of old. 'Surprised? Why should I be?'

He squeezed her arm, 'Perhaps you understand more than I thought. Anyway, add this to your data, Gerald is busy with a little art fiddle.'

Susan stopped outside her room. 'Will you answer one question?'

'Perhaps.'

'You've been to see Leigh's solicitor—who benefits under the will?'

He grinned. 'All three of them, directly or indirectly.'

'Aren't you going to do anything?'

He was pleased with himself. 'Just wait and see.'

To Susan's surprise and dismay dinner that evening was a family gathering; the Vanes were there and so was Edward. Perhaps it was gregariousness born of a common fear, perhaps it was simple curiosity. Outside, the wind had risen to a full gale and now and then rain lashed the windows. On such a night Roger Leigh had murdered his father and then gone downstairs to wait the coming of the mob that would have burned his house. Suddenly it was easy to believe that the Fates had conspired in a vendetta against the two families whose fortunes had been brought together in this estate. And here she was on the brink of a decision which would inextricably entangle her life with theirs. Edward sat opposite her and from time to time she was conscious of his gaze. He had a heightened colour and she wondered if he had been drinking. She hardly knew him; to discover him would be the work of a lifetime, his personality would reveal itself in a seemingly endless succession of layers each disclosed only by the penetration of the one before. She deliberately closed her mind to him and turned her attention to the others.

Gerald North, looking ill, toyed with his steamed fish. Lucy ate little but she scarcely raised her eyes from her plate, as though she wished to exclude everything and everybody; the barrier about her was almost tangible. Harold Vane seemed to enjoy his food and from time to time offered as conversational gambits comments or questions on the weather, the farms, Henry's work in the library, anything but the subject uppermost in all their minds. Beth was pale and withdrawn, deeply shocked by this latest and most intimate evidence that youth is no armour against the slings and arrows. Helen Vane's beautiful but usually blank features were troubled. Now and then she plucked surreptitiously at the plunging neckline of her wildly unsuitable dress, just in case she was showing even more than she intended.

Henry was watching them all and Susan was repelled by his detachment—clinical was the word for it. He looked at them as a pathologist looks at his laboratory mice. *Security is love*—she had read that somewhere and been impressed by it. All these people were insecure and how little love there seemed to be in any of them. 'Or in me!' She added in a burst of frankness, sounding the depths of her mood.

'I suppose we've seen the last of the police.' Vane made another attack on the intolerable silence, this time with greater success.

Gerald North pushed his plate away, just a fraction of an inch, and patted his lips with his napkin. 'I shouldn't think so. There will be an inquest on Francis.'

'Formality.' Harold dismissed the inquest. 'Don't you agree, Dr. Pym?'

Henry promptly disclaimed all knowledge. 'That is Mr. North's province, not mine.'

'I am not at all sure that the inquest will be merely formal,' Gerald said. 'It depends on the police and the coroner but in the absence of any possible proceedings in the criminal court they may feel the need for an enquiry more searching than usual.'

'But the police are satisfied.'

Gerald stroked one long bony hand over the other while Flossie served him with dessert. 'I doubt if the police are satisfied, although it is difficult to see what they can do about it. Their case, remember, began before Mei Mei was kidnapped, with the disappearance of the two girls and with certain evidence which suggested a link between the disappearances and *Peel*.' Gerald went delicately to work on an orange. 'I have no doubt that they fully expected to find the bodies of the girls in the chamber below the lake, but so far, I understand, their search has been unproductive.'

'But they are satisfied that if the girls have been kidnapped and murdered, Francis was responsible, and so, apparently, are we.' Edward was aggressive.

An uncomfortable silence until Harold risked, 'What else can anyone think?'

Edward said nothing to this but after a moment he went on in a different tone, 'Has anyone been allowed to see Mei Mei? They refused me.'

Beth Vane spoke in a low voice and without raising her eyes. 'I saw her for a few minutes this afternoon.'

'How is she?'

Beth's voice was scarcely audible. 'She was attacked and made unconscious without seeing anyone.'

They looked at each other embarrassed, perhaps because she had answered their thoughts rather than their words.

'She doesn't believe that Uncle Francis would do that to her and neither do I!' Her words merged into a sob and she got up and hurried from the room.

All their eyes followed her. 'Funny little thing,' Helen Vane said.

Edward half rose. 'Shall I . . .?'

'Leave her.' Harold was definite.

Another silence until the thought which had been troubling Helen at last broke surface. 'Does anybody know who gets the estate and the money? I mean, Francis must have made a will.'

Edward chuckled explosively, Harold flushed but Gerald seemed to take the question as reasonable and answered

163

without apparent rancour. 'I am not his solicitor but he never made any secret of his intentions, the bulk of the estate was to go to Lucy.'

'Lucy!' Helen's beautiful blue eyes widened in astonishment. 'Well I never! Doesn't anybody else get anything?'

Gerald was mildly reproving. 'Lucy is his only child, surely it is natural ... As to other bequests ...' He made a gesture disclaiming interest, 'they are the business of the people concerned.'

Edward poured himself another glass of claret. 'It's no secret that he promised to leave me ten thousand and the use of my cottage.'

Gerald's eyes came to rest on Harold and Harold shifted uncomfortably. 'He said that I was to have Ella's share in trust for Beth and Johnny. He mentioned it a couple of times but whether he did anything about it ...'

'You didn't tell me!' Helen was outraged.

'Because it was none of your business,' Harold snapped. 'The money would have gone to Ella, now it will go to her children. Now can we change the subject. This is ghoulish.'

But Helen was unperturbed. She faced Gerald again. 'What about all those antique things found in the mine, they must be valuable surely?'

'Fairly, I should imagine,' Gerald agreed.

'Won't they be treasure trove or something?'

Gerald allowed himself a show of irritation. 'The law on treasure trove only applies where it is not possible to establish the rightful owner of property found in this way. In this instance there can be no doubt that it formed part of Joseph Leigh's estate and is therefore part of the legacy to his heirs in succession. It will come to Lucy with the residue of the estate.'

Helen looked across at Lucy as she might have looked at a missed bargain in a sale, 'You'll be a rich woman, Lucy!'

But Lucy seemed as remote from the discussion as the man in the moon. She never raised her eyes from her plate and she never spoke.

But afterwards she served coffee in the drawing-room

while Flossie did the washing up because it was Sarah's night off. As they sipped their coffee there were long silences while everybody listened to the wind. With every violent gust the logs in the fireplace flared, sending a column of sparks flying up the chimney.

'This will bring down a couple of those dodgy elms behind the house unless I'm much mistaken,' Harold said. 'I warned Francis but he wouldn't listen.'

Gerald nodded, anxious to get the conversation off the ground. 'Awkward things elms, shallow rooting.'

'I wish the wind would bring down that bloody willow!' From Edward. He was already drinking whisky while the others finished their coffee.

North was indignant. 'Don't be absurd, it's a magnificent tree!'

Uniquely, Lucy volunteered an opinion, 'I don't like it, Gerald, I never have. Ever since I was a child I've hated to go near it.'

Gerald's irritation got the better of him. "Only because Edward filled your head with some nonsense about the place being haunted by dead miners.'

Edward grinned. 'Actually it was a poem that upset Lucy —something about a willow tree by a river and a lost spirit . . . '

Henry was sitting back in his chair, almost lying, his eyes half closed, his arms resting on the arms of his chair, elegantly relaxed. Now he murmured:

> 'Know ye the Willow-tree
> Whose grey leaves quiver,
> Whispering gloomily
> To yon pale river?
> Lady at eventide
> Wander not near it:
> They say its branches hide
> A sad lost spirit!'

'It's from a poem by Thackeray.'

Helen Vane shivered. 'Dr. Pym, you make me feel quite creepy.'

Flossie came. 'It's the Superintendent, he wants to see you, Mr. Edward.'

Edward looked startled. 'Me? Then you'd better show him in here, Flossie. We are a family without secrets.'

Superintendent Judd arrived, blinking in the light. Little drops of moisture glistened in his moustache and stood like beads on his highly polished toe-caps.

'A new development. Superintendent?' Gerald was almost jovial.

'You could say that, sir.' He looked round at the company. 'It concerns you and Sir Edward and Mr. Vane . . .'

Sir Edward! It had not occurred to Susan that the title would go to Edward. She was intrigued by the effect Judd's use of it had on him, a tightening of the jaw muscles and a quick frown. She could guess at the unspoken obscenity. Well, it was hard luck on a Comrade. Ironic too. Gerald would have loved it. Meanwhile Judd was going on just as though he hadn't dropped a brick. 'Is it possible for me to talk to you gentlemen somewhere?' He broke off, looking at Henry. 'It might be a good idea if Dr. Pym was there also. He has, I believe, been acting at the request of the family.' A questioning glance at each of the three men in turn. 'Sir Edward? Mr. North? Mr. Vane? I take it that you have no objection to Dr. Pym joining our discussion?'

They murmured something which could be taken for agreement.

'Perhaps we could go to another room?' Judd looked round vaguely.

'What's wrong with this?' Edward wanted to know. 'It's warm and comfortable and we no longer have secrets from one another.'

Judd shrugged. 'As you wish, Sir Edward.'

CHAPTER THIRTEEN

'Sit down, Superintendent. Make yourself at home. Drink?' Edward was high and slightly larger than life. 'It's all on the house.'

'No thank you, sir.'

Gerald stood on one foot, then on the other; perhaps he was uncomfortable because Edward was making a fool of himself, perhaps because he thought Edward was taking his place. As Lucy's husband . . . Harold knocked out the dottle from his pipe and started to refill. He seemed calm, detached.

Susan had convinced herself that one of the three was a murderer. Edward Leigh, Gerald North, Harold Vane—which? She was ready enough to believe in Edward's innocence but on what grounds? Only because she knew him better than the others. Logically he was probably the most eligible. Unstable, a woman chaser and permanently hard up. By comparison Harold was out of the running. A solid respectable citizen complete with pipe. Half the time he reminded her of Harold Wilson doing a T.V. commercial for the Labour Party. If he ever did murder somebody it would probably be Helen. Then there was Gerald. An introvert, emotions fined down to gossamer threads and all tangled up. But he was a thinker not a doer; a scholar shunted off into a siding. Henry had said that he was engaged in some art fiddle but that was a very different thing from murder. And it wouldn't be a money fiddle; more likely a faked claim for priority or a rigged find, something academic and bloodless.

Judd was pulling a lady's handbag out of his briefcase and she recognized the cheap imitation snakeskin. He held it up as a conjuror holds his rabbit. Gerald looked at it. 'A handbag? I don't understand. Is it supposed to mean something to us?'

Judd dangled the bag in front of Edward. 'Sir Edward?'
'I've never seen it before.'

'I think you have, sir. It belongs to Miss Lorna Field. She
identified it this afternoon.'

A little drunk, Edward was finding it difficult to make
the right responses and overdid it. 'I didn't recognize it. I
mean, one handbag is much like another. I don't suppose
I even noticed her bag—you wouldn't, would you?'

Judd looked at him but said nothing. Harold was irritated
or pretended to be. 'What's all this about, Superintendent?
What's it got to do with us?'

Judd placed the hangbag on the floor beside his chair. 'I
expect Sir Edward will tell us that.'

This was too much; Edward exploded. 'For Christ's sake
call me by my proper name! As far as the bag is concerned
it's simple enough in all conscience. Lorna Field is just a
girl I've taken out a few times and the last time was the
Monday evening before Christmas. My car was in dock,
Francis's wasn't in the garage, so I took Gerald's.'

A disdainful smile from the lawyer but no comment.

'Lorna telephoned me next day to say she'd left her bloody
bag on the back seat of the car but by that time, Gerald,
you'd taken the car to your office. I waited till you got back
in the evening, then looked for the bag but it wasn't there,
so I assumed the silly bitch had left it somewhere else. As
a matter of fact, Susan caught me looking for the bag—
or very nearly.'

Edward wasn't exactly gaining friends and influencing
people. Judd's disapproval was almost tangible. Gerald was
bland. 'Now that the young woman's property has been
recovered, Superintendent, I take it we can forget the incident.'

Judd turned placid spaniel eyes on the lawyer. 'The bag
was found yesterday afternoon in the room under the lake.'

'Ah!'

'Can you explain, sir, how it came to be there?'

North shook his head. 'No, I cannot.'

It was like watching a slow-moving television drama with
the sound turned down. Both North and Judd underplayed
168

their parts, avoiding emphasis. But Judd was persistent. 'Is it possible that you noticed the bag in your car and put it on one side until you had time to enquire as to its owner?'

Gerald refused this loophole, 'I did not see the bag in my car and I did not remove it.'

Judd turned to Edward. 'Mr. Leigh? Do you know how the bag came to be where it was found?'

'Not a clue.'

Harold cleared his throat. 'Surely it must have been Francis who put it there?'

Judd's unemotional stare was disconcerting. 'Why, Mr. Vane? Why should Sir Francis remove a girl's bag from Mr. North's car and take it to the room under the lake?'

A movement of irritation. 'How should I know? But you can take it from me that it would be quite in character for Francis to do just that if he thought he could make use of it later. In any case he was the only one with access to the underground room, wasn't he?'

The sixty-four thousand dollar question and Judd wasn't going to answer it just yet. But his manner was comfortable, reassuring. 'There are several aspects of Sir Francis's behaviour before his death which are puzzling. As you probably know, he did not drive to the hospital to pick up Miss Wong as he had promised to do. She had to walk home and, making for the Vane house, she took the northern estate road. When she reached the point where the road skirts the *Pinetum* she was attacked and rendered unconscious. She knows nothing of what happened to her from that moment until she recovered her senses in hospital. *We* know that she must have been carried through the pines to the lake.' Judd stopped speaking and looked round at his hearers. 'If Sir Francis intended to kidnap her why did he not pick her up as arranged and drive by the southern road, which would have brought him within a few yards of the timber bridge and saved him the mammoth task of carrying her down through the pinewood?'

Harold was faintly contemptuous. 'It seems obvious that he didn't want her to identify him.'

'Why not?' Judd put the question mildly. 'If he intended to commit suicide what could it have mattered to him one way or the other?'

Harold was dogged. 'Probably he had no intention of killing himself at that time.' Susan had the impression that he was mainly concerned to discourage the stirring up of more mud. Perhaps he had good reason, perhaps he really believed that it was all over.

'I see.' Judd seemed to treat the idea with respect. 'But in that case he couldn't have intended to kill the girl either. He must have meant that they would both return to circulation.' His eyes rested on Harold. 'Is that your idea, Mr. Vane?'

Harold hesitated. 'I suppose so, yes. I admit that put like that it hardly sounds convincing.'

Judd yielded to temptation and brought out his pipe and pouch. Everybody relaxed. 'No,' he agreed, 'it doesn't sound at all convincing, and less so if you remember that by offering to fetch Miss Wong he made himself *accountable* for her.' He paused to let the point sink in and to light his pipe. 'More remarkable, he made quite sure that suspicion must fall on him by telling Mr. North an entirely fictitious tale about a cable.'

Harold prodded the air with his pipe stem, reasonable but impatient, 'But whatever you say, you can't alter the fact that Francis was found dead in his room under the lake with Mei Mei beside him.'

Judd stared into the fire, nodding his head. 'I agree we can't alter that, but what we need is a better explanation of how they came to be there.'

Harold frowned. 'I'm not sure that I understand you.'

Judd stirred himself. 'Then I'll speak plainly. I do not believe that Sir Francis kidnapped Miss Wong, nor do I believe that he killed himself.'

At last Judd had nailed his colours to the mast. Susan looked round to judge the effect. None on the two women. Lucy had either not heard or expected what she heard. Helen, bemused by the discussion of pros and cons, had long since withdrawn into a simpler private world. Henry seemed more than half asleep. For the rest the tension was back and redoubled. Harold made an unconscious gesture, almost as though he were thrusting aside some physical burden. Gerald, his head on his chest, looked at the Superintendent from under contracted brows, shrewd, appraising. 'I suppose you could be right.'

'So he *was* murdered!' The most dramatic response came from Edward who had been sitting, sipping a drink, silent and morose.

'Murdered? Who?' Helen had been brought back by the most evocative word in the language.

Gerald took charge. He might have been conducting a case in court, his dry manner betrayed nothing of personal involvement. 'You are saying, Superintendent, that some third party was responsible for kidnapping the Chinese girl and that Francis was killed by that person in circumstances which would suggest guilt followed by suicide. Is that correct?'

'That is correct.'

'Then what about the other two girls? After all, it was because of their disappearances that your investigation was undertaken.'

Susan knew the answer Judd would give but apart from Henry and one other no one else could know. Judd was no actor and he took his job too seriously to dramatize it but his line was foolproof. 'Both the girls are alive and well.' He waited for comment but none came. Perhaps they were too astonished. 'Eileen Cassels telephoned the police station early this evening as a result of all the publicity in the press and on television . . . She and Gillian Ford are living and working in Notting Hill Gate.'

'So that their disappearance had nothing to do with *Peel*?' Edward demanded.

'Nothing.'

'Christ!' Edward laughed unconvincingly.

'What an irresponsible thing to do.' Gerald was angry. 'The misery and mischief they have caused in this house.'

Lucy reacted for the first time. 'Thank God they're safe.' But she added at once, 'They could have trusted me. You would have thought after all these years . . .' If Lucy ever kept pet guinea pigs they probably bit her.

Harold Vane got up to throw more wood on the fire. The hollows shells of burnt-out logs collapsed in a volcano of sparks and the new wood began to hiss and steam. Harold brushed his hands together and returned to his seat. 'I have never believed that the disappearance of those girls had anything to do with us.' He looked meaningfully at Pym. 'I came to the conclusion that the anonymous letters and the other nonsense we have had to put up with sprang from Francis's devious and unbalanced mind but if Francis really has been murdered . . .'

Lucy cut in and her voice carried a hint of hysteria, 'For God's sake let it lie! The girls are safe, Mei Mei is recovering and my father is dead. *He took his life while the balance of his mind was disturbed*—that is what they will say, let them say. Is there any point in torturing the living for the sake of the dead?'

Harold nodded. 'I agree.'

Gerald shook his head and kept on shaking it.

Edward was flushed and excited. 'But I don't agree! If there is a chance that Francis was innocent . . .'

Lucy laughed. 'But don't you see? If it wasn't father it was you, or Gerald or Harold. Father is *dead*!' Her looks were more expressive than words. Why not leave it at that? She turned to Judd, 'You come here stirring everything up again, what evidence have you got?'

Judd was sympathetic but unflappable. 'First, as I have tried to point out, Sir Francis's behaviour was quite inconsistent with the idea that he subsequently assaulted Miss Wong and took his own life. Second, the autopsy shows that he had taken a substantial quantity of a sedative drug. It is the opinion of the pathologist that he was probably unconscious when the bullet entered his brain. Third, it seems almost inevitable that whoever used that underground room for weeks or months must have left his fingerprints;

your father's prints are nowhere to be found.'

A new thought for Harold. 'What about other prints?'

'We found others.'

'Whose?'

'Do you suppose that you left your prints in the room, Mr. Leigh?'

Edward was preoccupied. 'What? No, I don't think so.'

'Mr. North?'

Gerald hesitated, 'Not as far as I can remember.'

'Mr. Vane?'

'No, I don't think so.'

Judd nodded. 'I shall have to ask you to allow one of my men to take your prints for elimination purposes.'

'Elimination! I like that!' From Edward.

'It's our new word, Mr. Leigh,' Judd said gravely, 'thought of by younger and abler brains than mine.'

'Oh, my God!' Lucy was near the limit of endurance.

'I need a drink.' Edward got up and went to the side table. 'Helen? Susan? Lucy?'

He poured drinks for them all except the Superintendent and Lucy. Susan had gin, Henry, unusually, had a whisky, Gerald asked for tonic water. 'I should like to hear Pym's views on all this,' Edward said. 'If the Superintendent has no objection.'

Perhaps this was the moment Henry and Judd had planned for. At any rate Henry rose with smooth alacrity to the occasion. 'If Sir Francis was murdered, and I agree with Mr. Judd that he was, there is no evidence to exclude Mr. Leigh, Mr. Vane or Mr. North from suspicion. Mrs. North has already made this point. None of them has an alibi and if Sir Francis did not kill himself it seems likely that one of the three was responsible for his death.'

Henry held up his glass so that the light was shattered on its diamond facets. 'Think what the murderer had to do, what he had to know, what he had to be. He must have known of the room below the lake. He must at some time after eight-thirty on the evening before Sir Francis's death have persuaded or induced him to go there. Sir Francis's car was taken out of the garage. It could be that Sir Francis set out to collect Mei Mei from the hospital but we know that he did not do so and that his car was found on the fringe of the *Pinetum*. Perhaps he was intercepted by the murderer at some point along the northern estate road and compelled or persuaded to go to the lake. Flossie did not actually see Sir Francis after eight-thirty so it is possible that he was taken to the lake well before ten o'clock and that it was his murderer who drove the car to the *Pinetum* to add colour to the idea of his guilt. The fact that the driving seat was adjusted to suit a taller man favours this possibility.'

It was astonishing, though Susan had seen it happen before. In a few sentences with the gravest implication for one of the three men, Henry had, nevertheless, succeeded in lowering the tension—earthing the charge. The identity of the murderer had become a subject for objective discussion. Susan had once attributed to him the ability to defuse an orgasm.

Henry paused to sip his drink. The wind had reached a new crescendo of fury and the heavy velvet curtains stirred uneasily. 'According to Mr. North, Sir Francis told him of a cable for Mei Mei from her parents in Malaya and asked him to get in touch with the hospital, which he did. But there was no such cable and if Sir Francis is innocent of kidnapping Mei Mei, why should he have invented one?' Henry allowed the question to hang in the air while everyone studiously avoided looking at North, but the lawyer seemed unperturbed. He sat, attentive, benign, perhaps slightly contemptuous, as counsel for the defence may listen to the prosecution.

'The question is whether Sir Francis himself was deceived by a third person into believing that there was a cable. Again, according to Mr. North, Sir Francis told him that the message had come from "the Vanes". In support of this we know that the telephone rang at about ten o'clock or a little before. Flossie says that she heard it just before going upstairs to bed and Mr. North says that he heard it while he was in

174

his bath. It rang only briefly, which suggests that it was answered promptly—we are to assume, by Sir Francis.'

Henry turned his gaze on Vane. Harold was sitting back in his chair, his pipe going well, the bowl supported between finger and thumb. 'That call could have been made by you and it would have sounded perfectly reasonable. "There's been a cable phoned through . . . I'm here alone and Helen has the car . . . I think that someone should pick Mei Mei up . . .".' Henry raised his shoulders in a shrug. 'There is no evidence to show how you spent the rest of the night except your own testimony.'

Helen looked at her husband in blank astonishment. '*Did* you do that, Harold?'

Susan had the impression that she would have thought more of him if he had, but all Harold did was to remove his pipe from his mouth and say, 'Don't be such a bloody fool, Helen.'

Edward was at the drinks table refilling his glass. He turned to Henry, 'And what about me? Don't tell me— let me guess!' In a faint parody of Henry's manner he went on, 'I am often at the Vanes', I might easily have telephoned as though I was speaking from there and told Francis the crap about a cable. And there is no evidence except mine as to how I spent the rest of the night. What a pity I didn't ask the little cow her name.'

Helen giggled. Gerald made a gesture of distaste.

Edward laughed. 'There then, we have it. Each of us with equal opportunity to kill Frankie, and as he was shot with his own pistol and we all had the same chance of getting hold of that, we all had the means, so let's look at motive.' He was enjoying himself and he glared round the group, pausing for dramatic effect. 'I stand to gain ten thousand little green men which is a lot of lolly. God knows I need it! Flogging the gems of contemporary art has always been about as rewarding as pill pushing in the Vatican and I have expensive hobbies.' He paused, then added, 'I didn't kill brother Frankie but when I come to think of it the fact surprises me.'

He gave Harold a long and searching look. 'But everybody knows that Harold's need is greater than mine. He has an ornamental but expensive wife, a family, no money of his own and a salary from the estate which hardly amounts to a respectable pension.'

Harold's expression did not change, he was not even looking at Edward but staring placidly into the fire.

'I think he owed Francis money though how he got it out of him in the first place is beyond me.' Edward waited for some response from Harold but none came. Edward grinned. 'He needs the money all right but will he get it? Five thousand in trust for each of the two children—what good is that to a poor man?'

Helen looked from Edward to Harold and back again, unsure whether Edward was playing the fool or making an accusation and trying to work out how it would affect her one way or the other. Harold knocked out his pipe and put it in his pocket. 'You're drunk, Edward.' He said it without rancour as though it was a matter of no importance. 'Be careful what you say.'

Edward laughed. 'Yes, I'm drunk, or to be more accurate, I'm on the way to being drunk and that's the best state to be in. If I had my choice I would spend my days half drunk but it's not on, for one thing it's too expensive and for another it won't work. Either you stop drinking and sober up or you go on drinking until you're too pissed to know. That's my problem. Anyway, where were we?' His eyes rested on Gerald. 'Ah yes, Cousin Gerald. Save the best till last! That's what Flossie used to tell us to do when we were kids, wasn't it, Lucy?'

Lucy looked at him with surprising awareness and smiled. 'Yes, she did.'

'Good old Flossie.'

Gerald leant forward in his chair, bony hands on bony knees. 'Don't you think it's time you put a stop to this exhibition, Superintendent?'

Judd looked surprised. 'Me, sir? What authority have I over Sir Edward?'

Edward grinned. 'Sir Edward! You hear that, Gerald? Head of the family and don't you forget it. Well, you had nothing to expect from Frankie, did you? He wouldn't have given you the time of day. But you are Lucy's husband and Lucy gets the estate, the money and all the junk from under the lake. And Lucy is a dutiful wife in all the ways that matter to you. There's every reason to expect that from now on you will be able to play the role of the eccentric gentleman scholar. And you'll play it well—I give you that much—if they let you get away with it.'

Gerald looked at him without expression and when he spoke his words were devoid of emotion, 'Are you accusing me of murder, Edward?'

Edward balanced his glass on the arm of his chair and stood up, a little unsteady on his feet. 'You know bloody well I'm accusing you and you know bloody well I'm right. The wonder is that I never thought of it until tonight. As long as Francis was alive you were on the end of a string and you never knew how long it was. Whenever you seemed to be establishing yourself—carving out a niche (good, that!) for yourself in this crazy household, Frankie would give the string a twitch so that you fell backwards on your metaphorical arse with every bugger laughing. You remember when you decided to have your flat redecorated?' He stood over Gerald laughing, 'You are a sensitive bastard, Gerald, despite all your scheming, and you should have avoided Frankie like the plague. He had the knack of spotting people's weaknesses and remembering them.' He paused reflectively. 'You had more than a good reason for wishing Francis dead but I never saw the logic of it until this evening. I think that it was all this business of kidnapped women which put me off. You've never been very strong on women, have you, Gerald? They've been more Frankie's line—and mine. If anything I've always suspected you of being a bit the other way, if you understand me, although it wouldn't surprise me to learn that you are impotent, Jerry dear . . .'

He broke off as the door opened and Beth came in. He stood for a few moments looking rather foolish, then went back to his seat without another word. Beth was pale but composed though her eyes were still red with crying. She made for a seat between Susan and her father.

'Are you all right, Beth?'

'Yes thank you, daddy, I'm all right now. I'm sorry I was silly.'

Gerald was still unruffled. 'A great deal must be excused to a man in drink but an accusation of murder goes beyond all reasonable licence. I do not have to prove my innocence to you or to anyone else, Edward, I do not even know if I can, but I see that I must make the effort in self-defence.'

Susan found herself in sympathy with the lawyer, who had borne Edward's outrageous attack with calm and dignity. She felt angry and contemptuous toward Edward.

Judd stirred. 'You are under no obligation to answer those unsubstantiated charges, sir.'

North smiled. 'For my own peace of mind, Superintendent.' He paused, then, having collected his thoughts, went on, 'I need to account for my time between eight-thirty when Flossie saw me with Francis in his room and midnight when she heard me come in. Unfortunately all that I did in that time rests on my unsupported testimony except for the phone call I made to the hospital at ten-fifteen. That telephone call divides the critical time exactly in two. What am I supposed to have done in those two periods of an hour and three quarters each? In the first I might have induced Francis to accompany me to the underground room. There, presumably, I drugged him and left him. Perhaps I also shot him at that time.' The irony in his voice was perceptible. 'At any rate I must have returned to the house to telephone at ten-fifteen. I have very little idea how long such proceedings should have taken me but I imagine that an hour and three quarters would have been sufficient. Some time later I set out again, this time driving Francis's car and I drove it to the northern fringe of the *Pinetum*.' He paused and smiled, 'I need hardly say that I did no such thing but this must have been the pattern of my behaviour had I been guilty. At the *Pinetum* I waited for the little Chinese girl. Now, my telephone call

178

was made at ten-fifteen . . .'

Judd made a move to interrupt but North prevented him. 'No, Superintendent, let me have my say. Surely I can claim the same indulgence as Edward?' A momentary spot of colour in his pale cheeks gave the first sign of any emotional stress. 'As I have said, I telephoned at ten-fifteen. If we allow fifteen minutes for the girl to get the message, change and reach the gates of the hospital, that brings us to ten-thirty. It is rather more than a mile from the hospital to the gates of *Peel*— say twenty minutes' walk—and almost another mile to the point where Francis's car was found. Allowing for the darkness and the condition of the track the girl could hardly have reached there before ten minutes past eleven. Now I am supposed to have knocked the poor child out and carried her through the *Pinetum* to the room under the lake.' He turned to Harold Vane. 'You are a powerful and fit man, Harold. How long would it have taken you to carry the girl through the *Pinetum* to that room?'

Harold hesitated. 'I don't know, I shouldn't care to have to carry anyone down that slope in the darkness but I suppose it would take all of half an hour.'

Gerald nodded. 'I doubt if I could have done it at all, but allowing half an hour brings the time to twenty minutes to twelve and I still have to get back to the house by midnight.'

There could be no doubt that he had made an impression by this objective analysis. He had avoided overstating his case and scored by his restraint. Judd, who had seemed indifferent to the exposition, now took a hand, 'I tried to tell you, Mr. North, that according to the pathologist Sir Francis died between two and eight in the morning, certainly not earlier than one.'

North raised his shoulders slightly but said nothing.

A silence. Edward, past the ebullient stage of his drunkenness, sat back in his chair, his chin half hidden by the roll collar of his pullover, his eyes closed. Harold stared moodily into the fire. Helen looked from one to another of the circle and wondered whether to speak and what to say if she did.

Beth looked at her father, her thoughts busy with questions she was afraid to ask. Lucy might have been a thousand miles away and Susan wished that she was anywhere but cooped up with these people among whom there seemed to be no bond of sympathy or understanding. She looked at Edward and wondered how she could have thought of him as more than an amusing companion with a brand of cynical well-spiced humour which she liked.

No one seemed willing to speak. Outside the wind was dropping, but reluctantly; wild gusts shook the windows from time to time. Henry had scarcely moved since Edward's outburst, now he began to speak conversationally as though this was any after-dinner gathering of friends. 'I called on Dr. Frere this afternoon.'

'What?' North was caught off balance. 'Dr. Frere? What about him?'

Henry was casual. 'We talked about non-ritual bronzes of the T'ang. It seems that he is an authority and he was particularly interested in your mirror.'

'My mirror?' Gerald's voice was scarcely audible.

'He gave me this.' Henry reached over and handed North the photograph Frere had given him. 'It's a photograph of the so-called *Shield of the Persian Hero Hamzeh*, taken when the Turkish government loaned it to the exhibition of Chinese art in London in 1936.'

North looked at the photograph. 'I don't understand.' He was barely articulate.

Henry seemed not to notice his painful distress. 'You will see that it differs from yours, there are two circles of running animals and flying birds instead of one and I gather that the diameter of yours is a little greater.'

Everyone's attention was concentrated on Gerald now for whether they understood the reason or not there was no mistaking the fact that the lawyer was agitated. He made an effort to compose himself. 'You persist in referring to *my mirror*, Dr. Pym . . .'

Henry cut in quickly, 'I should have said the mirror of which you have a photograph and notes in your portfolio.

Frere tells me that the Turkish one is unique, yet you seem to have discovered a companion specimen. Where is the original of the photograph, Mr. North?'

Gerald shook his head.

'Is it still where you found it amongst Joseph's treasures? Or is it in some safe deposit? Or is it in your room upstairs?'

North still silent moving his head from side to side like an automaton. Henry's voice low, the silence in the room lending clarity and emphasis to every word. 'My guess is that you could not bear to be separated from such a beautiful thing even for a few weeks. I am sure that when your room is searched by the police the mirror will be found there.'

North could find no words for the denial he struggled to make.

'The kindest thing which may be said of you is that you allowed a love of beautiful things to destroy you. Yet that would not be true for you were driven by an even stronger passion. You had somehow to achieve distinction—not just recognition but distinction—in the field of scholarship you chose to make your own . . .'

'You are not obliged to say anything unless you wish to but what you say may be put into writing and given as evidence.' Judd administered the caution in a practised monotone cutting across Henry's words. The others hardly seemed to know what was happening.

'What's all this about a mirror?' Harold demanded but nobody noticed him.

Gerald found his voice. 'I did not kill Francis. You have shown that I could not have done so.'

Henry sat forward in his chair. 'Because Flossie says that you came in at midnight and Sir Francis died after one o'clock?'

North nodded. 'That is one reason.'

Henry shrugged. 'She was lying.'

Gerald sneered. 'Why should she lie? Not to shield me—she has always disliked me?'

Henry looked at him oddly. 'She lied *because* she disliked you. By saying that she heard you come in at midnight she

181

thought that she was giving you ample time to do all that had been done.' He paused. 'If you doubt that you can ask her.'

North shook his head.

Henry went on quietly. 'You will say that you could not have carried Mei Mei from the northern road to the lake and I accept that. You did not carry her, you simply lifted her on to your horse. There are a dozen places on the track to the lake where hoof marks . . .'

'I ride there often.'

'No doubt, but on this particular night you were seen returning.' He spoke casually but Susan knew him well enough to know that this was his gamble, that he had played his hunch.

For the first time it seemed that North was roused to some emotion other than passive apprehension. 'Seen?' He twisted round toward his wife. Lucy was looking at him but her face was devoid of expression and his own expression changed slowly from puzzlement to acceptance. 'So she told you.'

'Mrs. North has told me nothing.'

Lucy seemed to come back from far away, she turned to Henry. 'But you are right, I did see him, on horseback, full in the lights of the car.' She pressed her knuckles to her forehead. 'Why couldn't you leave us alone? When Mei Mei did not die you should have been content. What they do to Gerald will not bring my father back!'

CHAPTER FOURTEEN

'SO SHE TOLD you.' The words spoken conversationally, without aggression, without surprise or even regret. From that moment North's attitude was one of calm acceptance, so that it was difficult to believe that he had grasped the reality of his position. All trace of anxiety gone, his manner was that of a man who having risked some small gamble, and lost, admits his disappointment with a wry philosophical good humour of the 'I might have known' variety.

Judd wanted to say, 'Do you realize that you will probably spend the rest of your days in gaol? Or in a mental institution?' Instead he said, 'You admit to shooting Sir Francis with intent to kill?'

It was a damn silly question and it made North smile. 'You cannot drug a man, shoot him through the roof of the mouth, and then plead absence of intent, Superintendent.'

Judd drew complex arabesques on his note pad. 'You know that you are entitled to have a solicitor present at this interview?'

'For what purpose? To make the contest more evenly matched? I can assure you that there will be no contest, Superintendent.'

He was right. He had seen that Judd was uncomfortable simply because he was refusing to defend himself, to put up a fight.

There had been a change of scene. They had moved to an inspector's office in the local police station. The bare functional simplicity of a modern office; a desk with two telephones on it and a wire tray; a couple of filing cabinets; two or three chairs, a wall map on the glossy cream paint and a hatstand near the door where a constable tried to make himself look like another piece of furniture. An electric clock with a seconds hand swept the time smoothly, tidily away. Twenty minutes past nine.

Henry was there, sitting a little way from the desk across which North confronted the Superintendent. Henry looked tired and worried, and he fidgeted in his chair. A stranger might have supposed that he was the nervous unfortunate suspect under the protection of his impeccably correct and imperturbable lawyer.

North stirred in his chair, perhaps impatient at Judd's procrastination, and Judd began his questioning.

'It was two years ago. Interest in the history of the estate and of the Leigh family led me to examine the contents of the chest.'

'With or without Sir Francis's consent?'

A wry smile. 'Francis would never have gratified any whim of mine. He made the excuse, when I asked him, that he had already promised Harold the exclusive use of the material.'

'Isn't it odd that Sir Francis was never sufficiently curious to examine the contents of the trunk for himself?'

'Not if you knew him. Francis was the most insensitive man alive. And he had no sense of history.'

'So you read the diaries.'

He nodded and turned to Henry. 'You can imagine my feelings when I learned that there might be a collection of Chinese *objets d'art* about which nothing was known . . . I was overcome with curiosity. I realized, of course, that it was extremely unlikely to include anything of archaeological interest—nothing from my own period, for example; but a discriminating collection made in the eighteenth century even of such contemporary work as found its way into Europe would still be of enormous interest and considerable value. And there was always the chance . . .' He broke off, his features softened by the recollection of this rare moment of anticipation, then he frowned and his voice became petulant. 'Surely there is a draught here, Superintendent?' He looked round toward the door, 'Is that door properly shut, Constable?'

'How long did it take you to find the secret entry?'

He shifted his position irritably before applying himself to answering the question. 'I had no difficulty for although Roger had written in his diary that he would never reveal the secret he left very clear instructions on a loose sheet of paper inserted between the pages.' His eyes lit up. 'Do you recall Edmond Dante's emotions on the discovery of the hiding place of the Spada treasure or Crusoe's finding of the footprints? I think I must have felt something of the same excitement and fearful anticipation when I first looked down that spiral stair. It was three nights later before I forced myself to go down the steps and enter the chamber.'

The strangest interrogation Judd had ever conducted. At times only the spartan surroundings and the constable at the door destroyed the illusion of a chat between friends. North's manner was more relaxed than Henry had known it and he emerged as a more likeable person until one remembered . . .

'The room became my retreat, my refuge, and for nearly two years I was content. The collection turned out to be of even greater interest than I could have hoped, mainly because of the mirror and a few other pieces—ritual bronzes.'

'All, probably, received as gifts from the Turkish Porte by Joseph's father,' Henry intervened for the first time.

North gave him a shrewd look. 'You are very acute, Dr. Pym, you seem to have realized from quite early on that *my* mirror must have had the same provenance as the *Hamzeh* piece.'

Now and then Judd put a question but for the most part North was allowed to tell his own story. He gave the questions when they came considered and courteous attention and then answered them, if not briefly, at least with relevance. A telly interview of the John Freeman era. Sometimes the silence in the room was broken only by the sound of cars swishing past on the wet road outside.

'As time went on I began to find myself in a position of intolerable frustration. With so much to tell, I could not speak.' He gave a little deprecatory smile and shifted in his chair, 'I confess to my share of vanity and much of the pleasure in my good fortune would have come from publishing my finds, discussing them with knowledgeable people of the calibre of Dr. Frere and generally broadening my contacts in this field of scholarship.'

Judd smoothed his moustache, he was uncomfortable; as a confession from a murderer this was too smooth, too rational, too bloodless. 'But surely you only had to tell Sir Francis what you had found and you could have published whatever you chose provided you did not lay claim to the articles concerned.'

The lawyer looked at Judd with great intensity. Until now his manner had been conversational, as though no great significance attached to what he said; now it seemed that he felt much depended on his being believed. 'If I had taken Francis

185

into my confidence he would have gone to any lengths to prevent me from deriving the slightest satisfaction or benefit from what I had found.'

'For what reason?'

'Reason? Francis needed no reason to humiliate people who were in any way beholden to him. It was a reflex response. You remember Edward's words? "As long as Francis lived you were on the end of a string and you never knew how long it was . . ." He was right. We were all in that position but the others cared less than I. Francis could make no real impact on Edward and knew it; he knew too that he could only go so far with Harold, who manages the whole estate with great efficiency for a pittance . . .' He broke off with a gesture of resignation. 'With me it was different. If there are born bullies there are also born victims. My life after my marriage to Lucy was one of constant frustration and humiliation.'

'Surely you could have left? Set up house on your own?'

He smiled. 'I had a choice? Yes, in theory I suppose I had. But leaving *Peel* meant devoting myself to my practice, making it more remunerative and neglecting my studies, giving up all interest in my discovery, which had become the principal object of living. You could say that an alcoholic or an inveterate drug taker has a choice on similar terms.' He waved his hand expressively. 'Some idea of what time and freedom meant to me was Francis's principal weapon.'

'So you made up your mind to murder.'

North did not flinch at the word but he shook his head. 'Not at first, my first idea was simply to punish him by giving him a thoroughly uncomfortable few weeks. What I hoped to gain by such a course I cannot say but hatred is seldom logical. I wanted him to know what it was like to feel insecure, I wanted to reduce him to such a state that he too would begin to wonder whether the ground he walked on was solid or no. If you like, I intended to play a practical joke on him of the kind he had delighted in the past to play on others.'

'The missing girls gave you the idea?'

He nodded. 'Yes. Their disappearance, the still remembered legend of Joseph's misdeeds, Johnny the deaf mute, and

186

Francis's reputation as a womanizer—I thought that it would not prove difficult to link them all together in the public mind.'

'And if the girls turned up safe and sound?'

He shrugged. 'Nothing would have been lost. My main trouble was that with the first anonymous letter, Francis was all for calling in the police and this would not have suited me at that stage. I was able to dissuade him only by suggesting that Dr. Pym should be invited to stay here on the pretext of going through the natural history records and books in the library.' He paused to arrange his ideas, and when he spoke again he addressed himself to Henry: 'It was shortly before you came that I decided to kill Francis, it was borne in upon me that nothing less would buy me the freedom I needed and, I think, deserved. I realized the great risk I was taking and the fact that my scheme has failed comes as no great shock or surprise to me. For a man of my age, it was now or never; only youth can afford to wait and see, and of course, they never do.' He passed his hand over his brow. Sitting there in the unflattering glare of the overhead light he looked incredibly pale, his skin translucent, a network of thin veins at the temples.

'Once I had decided that it must be done I gave a great deal of thought to the means, for my task was complicated by the fact that, for obvious reasons, I did not want it known that I had discovered Joseph's secret. It must appear that Francis had done so. What better could I contrive than that he should be found there having, apparently, shot himself?' A distinguished don putting a rhetorical question to a couple of privileged students.

Suddenly Henry, who had scarcely spoken, seemed to lose patience. 'So that it became necessary for you to convince me and others who might interest themselves that there was some substance in the anonymous letters; at the same time you must begin, discreetly, to focus attention on the old mine workings and the possibility of a secret room of some sort beneath the lake. It would have been a source of embarrassment if, having killed Sir Francis, his body remained undiscovered.'

North seemed more amused than hurt by Henry's brusque manner. 'You have described my predicament very accurately, Dr. Pym. And I can understand your chagrin for it must be confessed that you fell in with my plan in a way which I can only describe as helpful.'

Judd dared not look at Henry and North went on, 'You can scarcely be blamed for you were investigating a crime which had not been committed.'

Henry made no direct response. 'I assume that Gillian Ford lost her silver cross on one of her visits to *Peel*?'

'Shortly before she disappeared. I found it on the stairs, slipped it into my pocket and forgot about it. When I found it again it seemed a pity not to make use of it.'

'So you bought some girls' underclothing and arranged the escapade with my car.'

The lawyer smiled. 'It is a pity that it was all a necessary prelude to tragedy for I must admit to having derived more innocent fun from my various little subterfuges than I have had at any time in my life.' He actually chuckled. 'I thought that I manipulated the diaries with considerable skill, allowing you to find the crucial one in poor Francis's room almost at the very last—although, I confess, rather sooner than I had intended you to do.' He was silent for a moment, reflecting on his murderous preparations as a child may recall with pleasure the day of a special treat. 'The Thunder God was out of pattern but it was irresistible. I saw that it made you think and I was more cautious afterwards.' He looked up at the clock. 'A quarter past ten.' For a moment Henry wondered whether he was going to get up, hold out his hand, wish them good night, perhaps thank them for a pleasant evening.

Instead he sighed. 'Well, that's about all except for the business with the little Chinese girl. I regretted the necessity for that but as soon as I began to make detailed plans I realized that it would not be convincing if Francis was found in the underground room alone. He would have to be there with a woman—that would be in character and to the official

188

mind it would suggest a plausible motive—a last fling before putting an end to it all.'

The true brand of Cain is unassailable egoism. Given self-absorption to the exclusion of everything else, it is a small step to murder. Although they had known other calculating deliberate murderers, confrontation with such naked unconscious arrogance is always a shock, so that Henry and the Superintendent were momentarily at a loss.

'You had already tethered your horse in the *Pinetum* when you joined Sir Francis in his room at eight-thirty?'

'Yes, Jock was waiting for me.'

'And you persuaded Sir Francis to accompany you to the lake—how?'

'It was simple. For a man of his pretensions Francis was incredibly stupid. I told him that Edward and I had been walking by the lake and that we had come upon what seemed to be an entrance to an underground chamber. I said that I had left Edward on guard and suggested that he should bring his revolver and that we should investigate together. It worked like a charm. We stole out like conspirators and he didn't even ask why we had to be quiet leaving the house.'

'You used Sir Francis's car?'

'Yes.'

'And when you reached the lake?'

'I had the entrance open in readiness but of course Edward wasn't there. Francis was scared. I said that Edward must have gone down ahead of us and that we had better follow but, of course, nothing would induce him to go down those steps.' North smiled. 'Francis was an arrant coward bolstering himself up by adopting the postures of violence.' He paused, reflective. 'If I had realized that clearly before, it might have been possible to avoid . . .' He pulled himself together. 'I said that if he gave me the gun, I would go down . . .'

'But you didn't kill him at once.'

He shook his head. 'No, I induced him to take a sedative and left him there. I wanted to avoid killing until I was satisfied that my plan would work.'

'Then you returned to the house to telephone the hospital?'
Judd wanted to get it over.

'I did not return to the house.'

'But you telephoned . . .'

'Using the telephone in the Pavilion.' Henry was impatient
with detail he had already worked out for himself. 'First you
dialled the house number and allowed it to ring a couple of
times so that Flossie might conclude someone had answered
it.'

North said nothing.

'After an interval you rang the hospital and arranged for
Mei Mei to be sent home. You then drove Sir Francis's car,
adjusting the seat to your length of leg, round to the north
side of the *Pinetum* and hid it in the trees. You lay in wait . . .'

Judd glanced at the clock. 'You realize that we must get all
this in writing?'

'Tonight?'

'Tonight.' Judd sat back in his chair. 'I expect that you
would like something to eat first.'

The lawyer took out his antique silver pocket watch and
compared it with the clock. 'I will have a glass of warm milk
if you please and two cracker biscuits without butter.'

CHAPTER FIFTEEN

A soft spring day with thin high clouds and a pearly
light over the harbour, the blues reds and yellows of the newly
painted hulls scarcely distinguishable from their reflections.
Muted, fluid colours of a Cotman sketch. Henry sat at his
desk writing. Susan brought in the mail. She dropped a pile
of letters on the desk and kept one which she opened.

'It's from Edward. Shall I read it to you?'

Henry stopped writing and looked up but said nothing.

'Sweet Comrade,
    It is now four months since our happening at *Peel* and

190

the dust is beginning to settle. It occurred to Uncle Edward that you and Egg-head might be yearning for news of us so here is a report from your correspondent on the spot:

It seems that only Flossy really mourns for poor old Frankie but we are all grateful to Pym for getting him off the hook. Not that it can matter much to him but murder is a bad habit and despite some natural prejudice on Lucy's part it is probably just as well not to have a potential addict on the hearth, so to speak. In any case they have made Gerald librarian in his place of retreat and as he was never very strong on creature comforts it may not be too bloody for him.

Lucy seems to have a new lease of life and to judge from her book post she must be starting work again. Mei Mei is fully recovered and looks good enough to eat. I am trying to persuade her to sit for me (cerise) but so far without success. "Thank you, Mister Edward, but mother would not like it." All nice girls have mothers. And talking of mothers, Lorna, the girl with a handbag, is about to become Lady Leigh. She will settle for nothing less and lacking old Joseph's resources, I have no alternative. Anyway she has a good figure, or will have, *Deo volente*, when she gets it back.

Come to the wedding and have a laugh on me.

Ex-Comrade Ballsitup.

P.S. Lucy has persuaded Harold to have a tutor for poor old Johnny and she is paying for it. Let's hope it isn't too late.'

'He encloses an invitation to us both.'

Henry looked at her quizzically. 'Disappointed?'

'Not in the least. I hope he's met his match.'

'All the same, it's time you thought about getting married, Susan.'

'I have—often.'

Henry sighed and turned to the window, 'Then perhaps I should think about it too.'